THE *Billionaire* AND THE BIKER CHICK

D1213689

ROSE M. COOPER

Book design by Oliviaprodesign

www.fiverr.com/oliviaprodesign

Published by Oshun Publications

www.oshunpublications.com

OTHER BOOKS BY ROSE

Billionaire Series

Training the Billionaire

One Night with the Billionaire

The Billionaire's Bet

Titles Available As Audiobook

rosemaecooper.com/audiobooks

JOIN MY NEWSLETTER
GET UPDATES,
FREEBIES & SPECIALS
rosemaecooper.com/newsletter

PROLOGUE

She woke up in a cold sweat, her hand searching all over the bed for him, but she came up empty. Her heart skipped a beat as she remembered that he was never coming back. He chose to leave, but she was left with heartache. She rolled over to his side of the bed and inhaled his scent deeply. It had slowly begun to vanish over the six months since he left. There she laid, relishing in the pain as happiness had once again escaped her completely.

She wanted so desperately to move on, to find someone new, but she couldn't do it. He had been the only man in her bed for three years. Nothing made sense to her. How could a person just walk away from something so significant without even thinking about it twice? She should've known this was how it would have ended. After all, he had been at the florist all the time, and he never brought her flowers.

How could she have been stupid enough to believe he'd stay after all of the stories that circled about her and Zoe? She thought he knew her better than to take their words over hers, and yet, when he came to say his goodbyes, it hit her harder than a train. The depression clawed at her soul, making her skin crawl with disgust about herself. She wanted out so bad. She needed to escape the dark cloud that hung over her head and shield herself from the bright light of the sun. Still, instead, she pushed herself deeper into the pillow, hoping to catch another whiff of his scent before it left her as well.

The sadness had become like a drug, an addiction she couldn't shake, not that she had the energy to even try and fight it. So instead, she buried herself deeper in the sheets, hoping, praying that he'd magically come to his senses and find his way back to her, to them. Deep down, she knew it was foolish to hope. Every person in her life had made a point to tell her too, but it was much easier to hope than accept the reality of the situation.

Even her mother had grown tired of the pity party she lived in. Every day she would come over just after nine in the morning. While her mother was there, she would beg her daughter to get up because life was passing her by. She didn't care, instead allowing the sadness to consume her once more.

It wasn't until two months later that she got up and had breakfast like she did before the breakup shortly after the eight-month mark. She showered, and washed her hair, did her make-up, and got dressed in her favorite clothes. She was done grieving a man that didn't die. In her den of depression, she decided then and there that it was time to start living. Time to take back what was hers and time to fight for her own happiness. Even if it meant she had to lose everything in return.

She owed it to herself to live life to the fullest. On the other hand, she had no idea how to do it.

1

RETURN TO THE TOP

Hard? Hard didn't even begin to explain what Crissie felt as she stood staring at the wooden door in front of her. With shaky hands, she'd tried to unlock the door many times, and, as much as she tried to convince herself, the shaking was most definitely not because of the late winter weather.

The sun peeked over the roof of the bar as she stood in front of the wooden door and. Even then, Crissie could still feel the terrible cloud of depression over her head as it pushed her deeper into the floor. When she stood up that morning, she made a choice. She chose herself, and she decided her own happiness. Still, not even that could erase the memories that lingered in every corner and shadow of the bar.

Crissie had a lot more on her mind than she led on, and anybody that dared look close enough would see the pain that radiated from her eyes, that pain she did her best to hide.

"Stop being a pussy. Just unlock it already," the words

hung in the air for a moment as she reprimanded herself. Brief thoughts of returning to the safe haven of her bedroom flashed before her eyes, and she huffed loudly.

"No!" she spoke, her word loud and firm. A strong reminder that she needed to do this. Luckily for her, nobody was around to see her complete and utter mental dilemma play out, not that she would have cared anyway. With one final huff, she unlocked the big wooden door. She stepped inside, letting it swing shut behind her, effectively shutting her in with her memories.

There wasn't much of a change to the place. Alex had kept it exactly as she liked it, and for that, she was delighted. Because she didn't know if she could make another change to her life, no matter how small it might be.

Without a glance, Crissie sped past his table. Their table, as she made her way to the backroom to find her favorite lemon-scented bleach and other cleaning supplies. Crissie was a simple woman. Born and raised to ignore all of her worries and fears by finding a distraction, and her favorite was by far the art of cleaning.

"Not even here for two minutes, and you're already cleaning," Alex's voice carried over the empty room.

Many women would consider Alex to be a fine specimen, but Crissie never gave any thought to that. To her, he was just Alex. Alex is the reliable friend that would bail you out of jail at three a.m. or Alex, the one who would bring you chocolates and wine after a breakup. After all, he had done both of those things for her multiple times in all of the years they'd been friends.

Crissie didn't even dignify his comment with a response, only taking hold of the cleaning supplies and making her way back towards the front of the bar. Alex stood at the bar, an open Budweiser in hand, and, once she stepped out into the open, he motioned the neck of the open bottle towards her.

She shook her head in return. "Could you stop drinking away the profits?"

The jab was meant as a joke, and although the smile was evident on Crissie's face, she could sense something was wrong by the dark look that crossed Alex's face.

"What?" she asked immediately.

Alex tried to shrug it off, but knowing somebody, half your life has some benefits for reading expressions.

"Alex, what? You're scaring me," real worry laced her tone.

Alex reached behind the bar, picking up their favorite tequila and two shot glasses. Taking his sweet time, he poured two healthy shots, sliding one over to her before mumbling softly. Crissie couldn't hear what he said, but by his evident worry, she knew it couldn't be good.

Crissie gave him a pointed look, confusion evident on her face as she gazed between him and the clear liquor in front of her.

"We're going broke." The words were spoken so fast that Crissie could barely comprehend them before Alex swallowed his shot, pouring another from the open bottle.

"How?" Crissie swallowed the liquid the moment the words left her mouth, her cleaning supplies now wholly forgotten.

Alex didn't answer the unspoken question, only poured each of them another shot. With intense eye contact, they both threw the shots back, neither making a face nor looking away.

"The bar isn't as popular as it was. He who shall not be

named did a real number on the reputation of this place." He made a motion towards the rest of the room behind him.

"I'm so sorry, Alex," she didn't meet his eyes as she mumbled lowly, toying with her empty shot glass. Tears burned at her eyes, but Crissie refused to give in to them. She had spent more than enough time crying the last couple of months.

"None of that!" he commanded, reaching for her hands. "We will survive this too, Cristina Fox. We always do."

With a sly smile on her face and the tears still rimming her blue eyes, she met his. "Oooh, my full name. You must be serious."

Alex let out a small chuckle, giving her hands one last squeeze before he let go.

"Almost as serious as you take cleaning. Now chop chop, don't want the boss to be mad." With those words, he reached for the cleaning supplies and moved to the tables that lined the open space people often utilized as a dance floor.

Despite the tears that still threatened to spill, she followed suit and began spraying the bar top with bleach. That was one of the things she loved most about Alex. He could always find a way to make her smile.

The two of them worked in complete silence, diligently wiping down each table and chair before the rest of their crew came in. Every new employee of the bar found it odd that the two owners insisted on cleaning by themselves each day. Deep down, Crissie knew the only reason Alex insisted on it was that he loved being hands-on when it came to their pride and joy. After all, it was the perfect reminder of how they spent every afternoon when they were in high school.

Crissie couldn't help the worries that flooded her mind. She'd spent months at home, and that caused all of her bills to pile up. Crissie was deeper in the red than she had realized, and that made her return to the bar so much harder. Crissie knew things were going bad when Alex told her all of the cops in town stopped drinking there, but she never realized just how bad it actually was.

HIGH POWERED

"I don't know, man; I just need a break for a bit."

The man on the other end of the line laughed loudly into the receiver. "No, you need to get laid."

Reece ran his hand through his hair. He couldn't even deny it. They both knew it was true.

"Maybe, I could always find a piece of ass on my vacation. And I don't even have to be careful about it. There are no tabloids or paparazzi in the middle of nowhere, Texas."

Another chuckle came from the receiver. "From what I hear about that place, the only piece of ass you will be getting is that of some old-age home."

The man burst out laughing at his own joke. Reece wasn't amused and decided to change the topic altogether.

"The only thing I'm banking on for this entire two weeks trip is getting rid of the old and starting fresh. The first step to that is getting Megan off my back as soon as possible."

Reece trailed his hand down his face as he thought about the pending meeting that afternoon.

"Man, I told you that chick is bat-shit crazy before you

even went there and hit that ass," James mumbled in between his loud chuckles.

The obnoxious laugh still came through the phone, but Reece remained quiet as his head worked overtime. Maybe going to a vacation spot in the middle of nowhere was a bad idea.

"Maybe you should think about getting a trophy wife?" James's voice was somber now, something that Reece had heard very rarely in the years they'd been friends.

A deep frown formed on his forehead. "Don't tell me you've been talking to my dad," the disdain was evident in his voice. If there was one thing Reece hated, it was when people sold him out, especially to his father.

James was silent for a while. They both knew the answer to the question that hung thickly in the air. "I know I should, James," Reece started. "I know, it's just that I don't know if I have the strength for a woman's shit right now. Business is good. I'm happy where I am currently. Finding a wife to stand next to me solely for honorary purposes is a little shallow, even for me," he finished.

James remained silent for another few moments. "We both know the actual reason is that you want to bang your secretary."

The two men laughed as the scattered blonde burst into his office. "Reece...," she announced before stopping herself mid-sentence. "I apologize, Mr. Hunter. There seems to be a problem with the investors."

Reece resisted the urge to reprimand the assistant for her unprofessionalism as he clicked off the call with his friend. "What is wrong, Ms. Dixon?" The ginger-haired woman flicked through the stack of papers in her hands, flusteredly looking for the page that she wrote the information on.

"The investors, I mean partners, in Dubai, have scheduled an emergency meeting because of the financial crisis." The girl looked rather pleased with herself for getting the sentence out in one breath, but Reece was starting to lose his patience, and quickly too.

"What finance crisis, Ms. Dixon?"

The girl stared at her notes. Reece was against hiring her, but his father insisted, more than likely because he had hoped Reece would fall in love and marry her. He probably would have too. She was undeniably beautiful, and he was just a man. He'd pictured her in his bed more times than he cared to remember. There was only one problem with her. It wasn't that she was inherently dumb. She just had the impeccable luck of constantly losing documents or forgetting about important meetings. And he was sure that this meeting was no different.

"When is the meeting Ms. Dixon?"

With her eyes trained on the ground, she swayed ever so slightly. "I believe it started 5 minutes ago, Mr. Hunter."

Reece had always been a very business-minded person. After all, he had been groomed into the CEO position since he was 10 years old, so it took a lot out of him to not lash out at the poor woman that stood in the doorway of his office. Reece decided to follow in his father's footsteps and use humility.

"Thank you, Ms. Dixon."

It only took a few seconds for Reece to log onto the conference call. "I apologize for the delay gentlemen, I was otherwise occupied, but you have my undivided attention now." It didn't take long for the men to voice their concerns about a possible merger with Ridge Corp.

"Mr. Hunter, it has come to our attention that your company is facing financial difficulties, and we, as a collective, feel that will compromise the integrity of both our companies."

Reece resisted the urge to sigh. He'd been doing a lot of that lately, and that is precisely why this vacation couldn't come sooner.

"There is nothing to worry about, gentlemen. As you know, our stocks dipped a bit in the last week, but I have spoken to my advisors on Wall Street, and the trajectory of our stocks is already positive and upwards. An occasional dip is very normal, and I assure you there is nothing to worry about. I have your concerns at heart and this project being a success is my top priority."

The statement was neither true nor false. The stocks were on a plateau, and nobody knew exactly what would happen within the next couple of days.

Reece had more reason to worry than all of the other men combined. Solely because he had invested a lot of his own money into the company, he was currently losing money at an alarming rate.

The men started conversing in Arabic. Unbeknownst to them, he had taken years of Arabic in high school and college, and Reece was good friends with the royal family, so he understood every word. He wasn't feeling optimistic as they spoke. Their concerns were valid, and he knew the only way out would be to lie. After all, it was one of the keystones of a good business. Once the men finished their deliberations, they focused their attention back on him.

"Can you guarantee there will be no further drop?" The men stared at him pointedly, all of their eyes focused on him now.

Reece knew how these things worked. He studied business psychology long enough to know exactly what steps to take. He slowly relaxed his shoulders, lightened up his features, and tucked his hands out of view.

"Why gentlemen, of course, I can. Ridge Corp has never been stronger, and this merger will only make us all richer. I am in constant communication with Wall Street advisors. They have all indicated that we are already doing much better than a few hours ago. That was actually the previous commitment I attended to."

He wasn't lying, James was one of the top advisors on wall street, and he had proved that there was great promise in the stocks.

The men stayed silent for a few painfully long seconds before the oldest beamed a bright smile.

"I will take your word Mr. Reece," the old man spoke with a thick accent and broken English.

Still, Reece could understand the gist of things. Reece talked a bit more with them before signing off the call, another deal in his pocket.

There was only one thing that remained now before he could go on his well-deserved and long-awaited holiday. That was getting Megan off his back before he could even drive to the airport.

BEG, BORROW AND SOLVE

I t's funny how quickly one lie can spread like wildfire. Crissie wasn't oblivious to the stares she got when she walked through town. She especially wasn't blind or ignorant to the death stares the lady at the mortgage office gave her.

That's the thing about a small town in Texas. When your ex-fiancé is a cop, many people believe his side of the story. After all, who would give half a shit about the truth? Especially if the topic of conversation was the biker chick, who owned a bar? The line seemed to stretch for miles, and the lack of distraction did nothing to stop her mind from drifting to faraway places.

Since Alex dropped the ball on her yesterday, her mortgage was the only thing Crissie could focus on, even though it filled her with feelings of angst and fear. Strangely enough, she preferred it to the all-consuming sadness she had felt over her eight months of crying.

She didn't dare give any thought to the fact that she would've been on her honeymoon now or that they probably would have been trying for a kid. Time felt like it was slowed entirely down right now. The line was barely moving at all, and it was becoming harder and harder to focus her attention on something other than the thoughts that consistently tried to invade her senses.

It was almost an hour later when the secretary finally called her in. The officer that sat across from the desk was anything but friendly and, once he saw her name on the papers, his frown deepened.

"How can I help today, Ms. Fox?"

Crissie swallowed deeply before answering, "I need to request a bit more time to pay by installments."

The man flipped through the pages for a moment. "I see here that you are already four months behind. How will you pay that off first?"

Crissie felt like a train had hit her. "Well, sir, I will be able to pay off one and a half times my regular installment until I am up to date. My bar is going through a bit of a rough patch at the moment."

Clicking a few keystrokes on his computer, he answered, "I can arrange that."

Crissie felt the weight lift from her shoulders, but she knew a 'but' was pending.

"However, I should inform you that the bank will repossess your home if you miss another payment."

He finished his sentence, and Crissie could practically see the metaphorical other shoe drop.

The weight came crashing down on her shoulders again, and Crissie knew she had to do something to ensure that she didn't lose the one thing that connected her to her dad.

By the time Crissie returned to the bar, her anxiety had set into a full-blown panic. Alex stared at her quizzically as she rushed through the open door and past the few men that lingered in the bar.

"Rough day?" he opened and slid a beer over to her as she walked around the counter.

"Like you wouldn't believe," Crissie took a long gulp of the beer. "I might lose my house and car at this rate."

Alex didn't say anything as he stared at her. The silence between them was deafening, even with the country music that blared over the bar's speakers.

"I was thinking...." Alex started but promptly stopped mid-sentence to serve the men that crowded around the bar. "Maybe it's time to move on,"

Crissie snapped her head in his direction. Heaven knows she'd heard those words a lot recently.

"Not like that," he quickly added. "I mean from everything, this town, our bar, just everything."

Crissie stood dumbstruck for a moment. He couldn't really mean it, could he?

"You're joking, right?" she queried. The cold, distant look in his eyes told her that he was indeed serious. "Alex, no, this is our entire life right here. We worked so hard to get here."

Alex kept his eyes pinned on the countertop. It became clear that there was something seriously wrong.

"Alex?"

He stared straight ahead, utterly silent as Crissie helped a few clients.

Alex slapped his hand down on the counter. There was a pain in his eyes. "I feel like we're just going stagnant here. We're moving in circles. After everything that happened, don't you think it will be best?"

Crissie thought about it for a moment. "It would change everything though, and the bar?" Crissie didn't know what to say or do. She didn't want to leave her entire life behind.

Alex looked a little more hopeful. "We sell it, pay off

your mortgage, and sell the house. We can move anywhere you want. We could both find love somewhere else and be happy again."

For the first time in a while, Crissie could see just how much he was hurting too. He was always so busy looking after her that she never even realized just how much he went through.

"Are you serious about this?"

Alex nodded in response, "I'm sick and tired of this place, aren't you?"

Crissie gave it a thought. Life could be so much better outside of this place, away from the bar, away from her ex that was making so much trouble.

She started really liking the idea when the phone rang. "Crissie speaking. How can I help you today?"

Crissie could hear Alex snickering as he served customers. He always joked that she sounded incredibly fake over the phone. The tension between them had vanished like mist before the sun, but Crissie knew their conversation was far from over.

"Crissie sweetie, how are you, my love? Listen, I can't talk long, and I know you're busy, but your mom tells me you are facing a bit of financial difficulty?"

Crissie wanted to scream at the perky voice of her mom's best friend. It was difficult to not lash out, and anger seeped in her veins because her mom struggled to keep her mouth shut.

"I'm really fine, Aunt Layla. Really, I am. I'll have it sorted out soon." The lie slipped past her lips before she could stop it. A part of her doubted her aunt would fall for it. The woman practically raised her.

"I'm sure," the savage sarcasm ran through. "Luckily for you, I think I can solve your problem if you solve mine."

Skepticism ran through her veins. Her aunt wasn't exactly known for being the easiest person, and her help usually came at a cost. Crissie was desperate to keep her house and car but not desperate enough to fall into a trap. Especially not since her mother and aunt tried to set her up multiple times since everything went down eight months ago.

"What kind of help do you need, Aunt Layla?" Every inch of Crissie's being hoped this was an actual solution and not a blind date. Or worse, a date with somebody she knew.

"One of my instructors quit, and I need a person with a lot of knowledge that can work with clients. Who better than you and I will pay you the full salary for only morning shifts. Please, Crissie?"

Crissie was somewhat surprised at the request. She hadn't been on a motorcycle in years, much less taught somebody else to ride.

Before Crissie could manage to say no, her aunt continued. "As an added bonus, I will send all of the lessons to your bar. And I'll buy each person a beer. I really need your help."

Crissie found herself agreeing before she even realized it. Crissie didn't like the idea of spending several hours a day teaching rich kids how to ride motorcycles. Still, she knew it was the fastest and only legal way she would be able to make that much money in just a couple of weeks.

Despite all of her worries, one thought stuck out to her. Maybe this was her way out. Crissie explained the situation to Alex, but he seemed distant.

"And just like that, you want to stay here again?"

Crissie looked him square in the eyes. "This has been our home since we were born, Alex. You really want to throw everything away?"

Alex looked out over the bar. He was silent, and Crissie left it that way. There was no animosity between them, but Crissie was not about to beg him. She grew up here, and she wanted to stay here, even if it meant she had to lose everything in the process.

4

REFRESH

The meeting with Megan went as well as could be expected. Despite all of the worries Reece had, she had agreed to take one million dollars to leave him alone. The money didn't really bother him. Besides, it was almost nothing compared to what he already had in the bank. The only thing he was worried about was how much shit she could create if she spoke to the media.

That was one of the absolute worst parts of being labeled people magazine's most eligible bachelor. Reece stepped out of the apartment building and moved directly towards his waiting town car. He didn't even want to think about what his father would say if he saw him now. It was true that absolutely everyone in his life had warned him about Megan. Still, trouble was a flame, and Reece tended to be a moth in these situations.

The ride to the private airport wasn't long. Reece had decided to utilize the short journey in a very productive way. By reading all about the things to do in Wakefield, Texas.

The car had barely come to a stop when Reece stepped out, walking straight towards the steps of his private jet. Out of all of the things Reece had achieved in his life, being able to buy this private jet was by far his favorite.

Reece spent the majority of the flight sleeping. He had promised himself to only relax on his trip. Despite how much he loved his job and his company, this break was well needed. Especially after the year he'd had with multiple scandals plastered over the front pages of magazines. Then the vast amounts of money he lost when the stocks dipped.

Reece knew it would've been a better bet to stay home and deal with everything that was going on, but his father insisted on the trip. Reece absolutely adored his father, even though his father had pushed him to take over the business. When he was younger, it really bothered him. His father was more occupied with how well he did at Princeton high school and then Princeton University. He understood it now, though; he understood everything he had to go through to be where he is now.

By the time the jet touched down on the tarmac, Reece was wide awake and more than ready to have a great time. Without any hesitation, he got in his car. He drove to the Four Seasons Hotel conveniently situated in the middle of the picturesque little town. Reece came here often. It was a part of his bigger vision for a happy place, and it helped a lot that he owned the majority of the shares in this specific location. As Reece stepped into the elevator, a bright yellow flier caught his eye. Somebody had haphazardly dropped it in the hallway.

The flier was covered in beautiful pictures of a river and small cabins on the lake. Find serenity with The Olive Canyon Inn Motorcycle Tours. The thought of these tours intrigued him, even though he hadn't been on a motorcycle since high school.

Once he reached his suite, Reece dialed the number on

the bottom of the flier, and a very cheery older woman answered the phone. "Hi, I found your flier, and it sounds exciting. It states here that you offer lessons as well. What does that entail?"

The woman let out a soft chuckle, "Okay, sweetie, so this is how it works. You pay for three lessons. Depending on the time of the day you'd like these lessons, I'll assign an instructor to you."

Reece listened intently to the instructions the woman gave him, taking mental notes as she listed all of the benefits. He had to admit that the woman was doing a very great job convincing him that he needed this motorcycle trip in his life.

"After your lessons, you will join a group of other people and drive up to the Olive Canyon Inn, where you will spend four days and then drive back and return the bike."

Reece went quiet as he decided, and when he agreed, he learned that he'd start lessons with the next group the following week.

"That's great, sweetie!" The woman suddenly exclaimed.

She was so loud that Reece had to move the phone away from his ear. The woman proceeded to give him directions to a bar not too far from the hotel and explained what he should do once he got there.

After the phone call, Reece ordered in-room service. The service was spectacular, and not even 30 minutes later, the Chicken Caesar salad was on a trolley in his suite. Reece dove right in, pouring the salad dressing liberally on the salad. As he started eating, his phone rang. This time his father was on the other end.

"Hi Dad, what's up?" he replied as he placed the phone on speaker and put it on the trolley in front of him.

"You fly alright?" A small smile graced Reece's face.

He'd learned a long time ago that was the way his father showed he cared. "Yeah, how are the stocks looking?"

This was the way all conversations played out between him and his father. There was no emotions or actual conversation. Work was their middle ground, and it dominated each and every conversation the two ever had.

"Slowly but steadily rising, you sure are a lucky man. Those investors would have pulled out for sure if the stocks remained that terrible."

Reeces swallowed his food and, with it, huge relief. The situation could have turned out much worse, which meant his money would be refunded within the next few weeks.

Before Reece could say a word, his father continued, "I'm actually just calling to let you know the deal went through. We officially own one of the largest retailers in America."

This time a full smile appeared on Reece's face. This meant more credit to his name and more money in his pocket. The company would also now be the second richest, right after Amazon.

"I have golf. Enjoy yourself but stay out of the tabloids."

With that, his father clicked off the call and left Reece staring at his phone intently for a few minutes. What did his father think he was going to do?

After he finished his salad, Reece made the short drive to the bar the lady had told him about. The bar was mildly busy but not nearly as much as he was accustomed to. Inside of the bar, he met a man called Alex, who graciously helped him complete the documents needed for the training to commence.

Across town, Crissie is sitting in her car, again deliberating with herself. Right outside her car is the town florist. Crissie had only been inside a few times. The majority of those times were in the last eight months. She hated herself a little more each time she entered the shop, but today was different. Today would be the last time she'd submit herself to this torture willingly. Crissie stepped out of her car and made the short walk to the storefront. Inside, she looked around for the familiar raven-haired woman.

The woman stood against the building's back wall, with her jet black hair and gray eyes. Her frame was short, and she was very skinny. Overall, she was everything that Crissie was not.

The first time Crissie had entered the shop, she had hated the woman. Crissie didn't even know her name, but she did know that she was one reason her engagement ended the way it did. As Crissie stood admiring the beautiful red roses, she didn't feel that kind of animosity towards the woman. In fact, Crissie didn't feel much of anything,

At that moment, Crissie realized she'd begun to make peace with everything that went down. Crissie left the florist with a new pep in her step. She clutched onto the red roses she'd bought for herself and made her way back to the bar.

In the parking lot, Crissie almost hit another car that was in her spot. She felt very annoyed at the sight and waited as the man slowly backed out of her spot.

"Did you just see that!" she exclaimed when she entered the bar a few minutes later. "The audacity of that man. Who parks in a reserved spot? Idiot!"

Crissie was in full-blown rage now. She'd erected a plate in front of her stop that clearly stated it was reserved, and the stranger just completely ignored it.

"Who was that idiot? Give me a name, and I will call him and give him a piece of my mind. This is fucking unbelievable."

Crissie continued on her rant. Some of the men in the

bar had also started watching her explode. Midway through a sentence, she realized how hard Alex was trying to keep his laughter at bay.

"What?" She snapped at him, causing him to burst out laughing.

"That 'idiot' is your first client." Alex kept laughing as he used air quotes as he said, idiot.

Alex handed her the completed forms through the laughter, and Crissie could feel her cheeks get hot. She had made such a fuss about him, and now she would be forced to spend several hours every day for two weeks with him.

Crissie was more than just embarrassed because of her entire episode. She was frustrated as well. Any guy that had the audacity to park in a spot that wasn't his was bound to be an insanely difficult client. Crissie just hoped that he had more brains when it came to learning than he did for reading.

5

FROM BAD TO WORSE

oday was not going to be a good day. Crissie hadn't had many good days since her break up, but she always made a point to be positive. However, today was not one of those days.

Crissie woke up with a pounding migraine. After spending most of the night awake, she felt the need for something positive. A few things in life made Crissie truly happy, and the top of that list was by far having dinner with her mother.

Her mother had been strong since her father died a few years ago. Her mother was there for her through all of her mistakes and accidents. Her mother had been her rock through the most significant accident she encountered. Without judging her once, her mother had held her hand every step of the way.

Once Crissie reached her mother's house, the happy and energetic five-year-old came bounding out. The little girl was the spitting image of Crissie except for her beautiful burnished brown hair. At one time, Crissie's hair was almost black. She assumed that the features must've been passed on from her dad. Crissie got out of the car and hugged her daughter. She had missed her terribly in the months that she had to live without her daughter.

Since Crissie was in one of the worst depressive episodes of her life, Crissie and her mother had decided it would be absolutely best for the little girl if she stayed with her Nana until her mother felt better.

"Hello, my love. How's your day been?" The little girl giggled as her mother tickled her mid hug. "Good Mommy, Nana took me to the movies, and we had ice cream for dinner." The girl's eyes suddenly went wide as she leaned close to Crissie's ear, "Nana said it's a secret. Shhhhhh."

Crissie winked as she picked the little girl up and greeted her mother, who stood on the porch. "Hi, mom," Crissie kissed her mom on the cheek as she stepped onto the porch and set Zoe, her daughter, down.

Crissie's mom poured two glasses of red wine and handed Crissie one. Crissie had to give it to her mother. She saw right through the happy facade Crissie worked so hard to perfect. In the living room, Crissie sat on one couch with Zoe on her lap. Crissie had learned early on how to juggle a glass of wine and a super active five-year-old.

Zoe was relaying all of the plans she and her grandmother had made for her birthday in a couple of months. Crissie was listening intently when she caught her mother's gaze. She knew the two of them had to talk.

Crissie spent another few moments listening to her daughter. "Baby, why don't you go play while I talk to Nana?"

Crissie smiled at her daughter as her mother sent her upstairs. Zoe looked at her mom intently. As she hugged Crissie, she whispered lowly, "you're in trouble," and with that, she bounded up the stairs giggling loudly.

"How are you?"

Crissie used to despise the question. She always felt guilty for still being heartbroken. Things were different now. She didn't feel heartbroken anymore. People always told her she'd just wake up one morning, and the hurt would be less, and she refused to believe it.

"I'm okay, honestly. Things were hard, but I'm good now. I agreed to start working for Aunt Layla, so I will be okay financially too."

Crissie took another mouthful of her wine. Just as she was about to ask her mom if Zoe could move back in with her, her mother started.

"I think it best if Zoe stays with me until you're on your feet again. I know you're strong, but I don't want Zoe to stress you out more. Especially not when you'll be working so much the next couple of months."

Every inch of Crissie's being wanted to argue. She wanted to scream and shout and demand her daughter be with her. Still, ultimately she knew it would be best if Zoe stayed here. Her mother could be there for Zoe in a way that Crissie could not at the moment, especially since her father didn't even know about her.

Crissie only nodded, drinking another sip of her wine. The two women spoke about everything that was going on in their lives. They talked about her mother's book club, and Crissie spilled the beans about her new client.

As she recounted how she freaked out because the client had taken her reserved parking, she felt a bit dramatic, but her mother burst out laughing at her antics.

It was barely a few minutes later when her mom called Zoe down, and they sat at the table for dinner. The pasta smelled delicious, and it went down incredibly well with the red wine. While they were eating, Zoe told her mom all about school and the boy in her class that pulls her hair at recess.

Zoe couldn't help but smile at everything. The day had been terrible up to now but, as she sat around the table with her mom and daughter, life felt good, and she was happy. Truly, deeply, and completely happy for what felt like the first time in years.

At that moment, Crissie didn't care about anything other than the little girl that was talking animatedly while clutching her fork tightly. Crissie remembers her labor, the first few months of the little girl's life, and, at that moment, she just felt undoubtedly thankful for what she had.

Having Zoe stay with her grandmother was Crissie's idea, and in the beginning, it was hard for all three of them. Her mother had to adapt to having a child in the house again, and Crissie had to adapt to being alone. Crissie never told her mother the whole reason why she insisted Zoe stay here.

Her mother assumed it was to give her the space she needed to work through the break-up. Still, in reality, it was because Crissie needed time to piece herself together again. When the break-up happened so unexpectedly, depression hit Crissie hard. It crashed over her like waves and pulled her under into a bottomless and dark pit. There were days that Crissie didn't think she'd make it out alive.

Her biggest fear was having her daughter find her if she lost the battle, and she didn't regret making that decision once. As Crissie sat reminiscing in complete silence, her mother topped off their glasses of wine. Even the old lady could see how much better her daughter was doing.

"Mommy, will you read me a bedtime story?" The little girl was the epitome of innocence, and she had such beautiful manners.

"Sure, baby girl."

Crissie felt pride swell in her chest as the little girl got off her chair and placed her plate in the sink. She then walked around the table and kissed her grandmother goodnight. Crissie got up from her chair with the ghost of a smile playing on her lips as little Zoe took her hand and led her upstairs to her bedroom.

Once in the bedroom, Zoe put on her pajamas and led her mother to the bathroom, where she brushed her teeth. Zoe had never been a difficult child, and she never argued or fought against her mother or grandmother. The little girl then got in bed and handed her mother a book about Beauty and the Beast.

"... and they lived happily ever after."

Zoe had fallen asleep halfway through the book. And Crissie had continued to read the entire story. After all, she felt that would be the only way to have a happy ever after. Crissie tucked Zoe into bed and kissed her forehead before making her way downstairs, only to find her mother fast asleep on the couch.

Crissie threw a blanket over her mom and locked the door behind her as she made her way out. A rattling noise came alive as Crissie started up her car, but she didn't pay any attention to it. Crissie was about halfway home when the noise intensified, and although she promised herself she'd get it fixed, the car gave up and died a few seconds later.

Crissie stood at the edge of the road staring at the billows of smoke that escaped the hood of her car. For a moment, she felt like life was completely against her being happy. With that thought, Crissie turned around and started walking towards her home.

Crissie had made sure to call a tow truck before she set

out for her walk. As there was nothing of worth in the piece of shit, she left her keys on the front tire. The walk was tedious and long. The further she walked, the more she despised the car. Crissie longed to be able to buy a new car, but she knew damn well that it would cost her more than she could save up. So, for now, she was stuck with that car.

As Crissie walked, she jokingly stopped at the wishing well. With a single quarter, she wished for a miracle. And then continued her walk back to her house.

6

FURIOUS FAMILIARITY

Everyone knew that Crissie hated working alone at the bar. When she and Alex opened the place four years ago, that was her only request. Since then, they implemented a schedule, and she'd never worked alone since. Today was different. Alex had come down with a stomach bug and had to call out, and since nobody was scheduled for the day, Crissie was all alone.

Luckily the bar was never busy this early on a Tuesday morning, and only a few regulars would come in, or so Crissie had hoped. She'd been cleaning for a while when a man came in and sat down in front of her. The man was objectively attractive, and something in Crissie stirred when they made eye contact.

"I should come here more often. It's almost like the best parking spot was reserved especially for me."

A sudden and uncontrollable rage filled her.

The man continued, "It's very convenient. I should really thank the owners."

A part of Crissie really wanted to lash out. Luckily for

the man, she remembered that she was indeed one of the owners, and she needed to show a little restraint.

"Well, I'm happy we could accommodate you," Crissie put on her flirtiest smile as she leaned on the bar counter with a dishtowel in hand.

Reece had woken up that morning feeling very excited for what the future was holding. He'd had a good conversation with his dad, and their stocks had almost completely recovered after the shit show when it dropped. The investors in Dubai had allowed the merger to go through. The week and some odd days he'd been on vacation have gone very well and today was the day he'd start his motorcycle lessons.

As Reece sat in the bar, staring at the feisty woman in front of him, he felt a bit of familiarity between them. He could've sworn he had seen or met this woman somewhere.

"Reece Hunter, he introduced himself. "I won't mind if you accommodate me." Reece held his hand out as he dipped his gaze lower as he spoke.

"Cristina Fox, the pleasure would be all mine." Crissie shook his hand, her rage still boiling heavily as she feigned interest in him.

Crissie could feel his gaze burning into her exposed skin as she bent down to grab a beer for the men that stood and waited patiently. Crissie took the money and handed them a receipt before she turned back towards Reece.

"What can I get for you?" she asked.

Reece let his gaze sweep over her again, and goose bumps spread over her skin everywhere his gaze landed.

"Are you on the menu?"

Crissie refrained from laughing. She just winked and grabbed a shocking pink highball glass. Crissie quickly assembled the drink in the cocktail shaker, adding in the vodka, peach schnapps, and orange juice.

Reece kept his eyes locked on her as she vigorously shook the cocktail shaker, poured the drink into the glass, and topped it off with cranberry juice. Crissie placed a cherry on top of the drink and slid it over to Reece.

He stared at her, puzzled as the glass stood between them. Crissie leaned forward and gave him a good view of her cleavage as she reached over and took the cherry by the stem, making sure to not touch the liquid contents of the drink.

Crissie popped it, placed it in her mouth, and took a few seconds to tie the cherry stem with her tongue. Reeces watched her intently as she took the tied stem out of her mouth and placed it in between them on the counter. "

I am. I come with *Sex on the Beach*."

With that, Crissie walked to the end of the counter and started serving the customers there. Reece flicked his eyes between her and the tied cherry stem. Reece was completely dumbstruck at the short conversation the two had just had. Never in his 28 years on Earth had he experienced such a fiery woman.

Reece slowly took a sip of the vibrant cocktail and was pleasantly surprised by the taste. He'd always been more of a Bourbon on the rocks type of guy. Reece keeps his eyes pinned on her as she serves the other clients in the bar. For a moment, he was so entranced by the beauty of her that he completely forgot why he actually came to the bar in the first place.

Crissie wrapped up a conversation with one of the regulars, handing him his old-fashioned, and walked back to Reece, who is now quietly watching her as he drank from the shocking pink highball glass. The view was very comedic. There was a silence between them, both of them just focusing on each other. Nobody could deny the apparent tension and attraction that hung in the air.

"Do I know you? I feel like we've met before," Reece suddenly asked.

Crissie blinked a few times. Her past was a bit checkered, and she hoped that he was mistaken. "I don't think so," she answered, "I'm certain you're not the type of guy someone would forget easily." She had a coy smile on her lips. "What brings you here today?"

Reece kept staring at her, forgetting to process her question as he tried to place her in his memories.

"I am supposed to start motorcycle lessons today. It's apparently a massive tourist attraction in this part of town."

Realization dawned on Crissie and, with it, a sense of disbelief. Reece was her first client for the lessons, and, just as she had feared, he was her only client. Alex had mentioned it a few days ago after he had signed the man up. It must have completely slipped her mind and, after all of her innuendos, it was going to be a long few lessons.

7

ALL THOSE YEARS AGO

"Fuck, I completely forgot about that. I am your instructor." Crissie wished the ground would open up and swallow her.

Reece's smile grew wider, and he became a lot more excited for his lessons. Reece could see her internal battle clear as day. Her fiery attitude was wrapped in a ball of rage, and he could swear they had met before.

"Hold up, we have met before."

Crissie felt embarrassed. She'd so openly flirted with the man, and now he was sure that they knew each other. She wished Alex was at work today. That way, he would have dealt with the man, and she wouldn't be so absolutely brazen and embarrassed.

"I doubt that pretty boy." Crissie wanted to kick her own ass. She couldn't stop flirting with him no matter how hard she tried. At this stage, it just happened naturally. Crissie could feel the way he judged her as his eyes roamed over her body.

She hoped that Reece was mistaken, that their supposed meeting was nothing more than a figment of his imagination. A spark of recognition danced in his eyes and, at that moment, Crissie realized she was fucked beyond belief.

Reece could see the rage and embarrassment that radiated off Alexis. As the memories of their encounter became clear, Reece felt heat spreading through his veins. "You really don't remember me, Crissie?"

The nickname chills her blood. Only people that know her call her by it. She rarely introduced herself with that name, and today was no different. Crissie knew for a fact that she only ever referred to herself by her nickname when she was drunk, and she hadn't been out drinking in five years.

"I'm afraid I don't." Crissie was reluctant to continue the conversation. She had no idea where this man came from, and she was a little scared to find out. Crissie worried that they knew each other from her drinking days, back when she was just a kid and none of the conversations she ever had about those days turned out good.

"I guess I am easily forgotten, but you, my dear, are not."

With his words, Crissie started to get an idea of where they knew each other from. Crissie gazed around the bar and became aware that the few regulars had already left, and she was alone in the bar with Reece.

"I could never forget the woman that walked up to me in the middle of a club and grabbed my ass, only for that same woman to insist that she'd be taking me home."

The level of embarrassment Crissie felt went through the roof.

"You look different now, though. Back then, you had electric blue hair. Then again, that was probably five or six years ago. The black hair suits you better."

Crissie subconsciously touched her long black locks. She'd loved the blue hair so much, but when she got pregnant with Zoe, she had to stop coloring her hair and she just never picked up the practice again.

"I don't recall that night. I must've been a little drunk."

They both knew Crissie was lying. She just prayed that was all he remembered from that night because the parts she remembered were very hot.

"I assure you that you were more than capacitated," Reece started. "I mean, we got in my car that night. I'm certain a part of my soul left my body as you wrapped your lips around my..."

Reece didn't finish his sentence. He only dipped his eyes down to his crotch, a smirk on his lips.

"Nope, don't remember it at all. Sorry."

They both knew Crissie was lying through her teeth. She didn't want to give him the wrong impression. Truth be told, Crissie hadn't been with anybody for just one night since Zoe was born. Crissie hadn't been with anyone at all for almost a year.

"Really?" he questioned. "Maybe then you might remember the ride up to my suite? After all, the hotel staff did bring your panties to me the next morning."

Crissie shook her head.

Another lie, he subconscious taunted.

In reality, Crissie did remember the situation. He had slipped his hand under her dress and removed her thong in the elevator. The thought returned a bit of anger to her body. That had been her favorite pair of underwear.

Reece stared at her. He could see the recognition flash in her eyes and the way she clenched her thighs together as the memories invaded her thoughts. Crissie couldn't even try to deny the way the thoughts impacted her. Crissie found herself remembering every detail of that night, as well as everything that came afterward, and within seconds she felt wary of Reece again.

"How about the way I wrapped your hair in a fist as I..."

"Okay, let's not go that deep," Crissie exclaimed suddenly. As much as she loved the feeling the thoughts had, she did not want him to say it aloud.

Reece let out a loud chuckle as he ran his hands through his hair. "That's most definitely not what you said that night." Crissie raised her eyebrows at him as a warning. "Holy shit, you are even hotter than I remember."

Reeces leaned back on the barstool as he took in her form for the umpteenth time that day.

"I can't do your lessons," she spoke again.

"Why?" Reece questioned, disappointment filling him. He didn't have any expectations of sleeping with her again, but he would've loved to see her straddling a bike and pressing up against his back as she showed him the ropes.

"I am alone in the bar today, and nobody else signed up for this week. I will redirect you to the other instructor, and you can join his existing class."

Reece was heavily disappointed now, but he didn't allow it to show at all.

"What if I want you to teach me?"

Crissie looked at him square in the face until she caught a couple of men coming in for their lunch drinks in her peripheral vision. "I'll be right back," Crissie turned to walk but hesitated for a second. Tapping on the counter as she walked away from him.

Reece followed her with his eyes as she greeted the men and asked what they wanted to drink.

He took a moment to reflect back, and the only thought that consumed his mind was how much he would love to have her in his bed again. Reece could vividly remember every detail of that night, and the reminder of how great she was in bed did not escape him.

As Reece sat and swallowed down the last of his cocktail. A brilliant plan started forming in the back of his mind. And boy was it going to be glorious.

8

HOW TO CREATE A PLAN

"Don't whistle at me. I'm not a fucking dog!"

Reece is suddenly pulled from his fantasies about Crissie when he hears her voice raised towards the two older gentlemen. The men snicker at her furious demeanor as they continue to whistle at her.

It didn't take a genius to figure out the men were already a little drunk or that Crissie was more than a little annoyed with the men as she stood slicing a lemon for their drinks. Reece sat at the bar and watched the situation intently. He wasn't inherently an aggressive person, but he was more than willing to step in if Crissie needed it. Although something in him was confident that she would not need any help.

"You might not be a dog, but that pussy is surely great."

Before Reece could get up to escort the men out, Crissie snapped. She slammed the tip of the knife into the counter in front of the two gentlemen.

"One more fucking comment and I will garnish this drink with your balls!" Crissie grabbed the knife and pulled the tip out of the counter. She pointed the blade at the two men, "understood?"

The men stared at her, fear radiating from their forms. They both nodded.

"It will be 12 dollars for the drinks and 18 dollars for the shitty comments. Your total is 30 dollars." Crissie slid the two drinks over to them and kept her open palm on the counter so they could hand over the bills.

One of the gentlemen placed a 50 dollar bill in her hand while apologizing for the inappropriate comments.

"Keep the change, dear," the man ended as they stood up to move to a different table. Crissie rolled her eyes at them as she completed the transaction and handed over their receipt.

She placed the remaining 20 dollars in the tip jar and reached for a bottle of Bourbon. As she walked over to Reece, she put the bottle down on the counter and reached for the first aid kit. Reece watched her intently as she poured some of the Bourbon on a bright red cut on her finger before swallowing a big gulp of the alcohol.

With one hand, Crissie tried to open the kit so she wouldn't get any blood on the fabric. Without a word, Reece reached over and helped her. Once it was open, he took out a Band-Aid and waited for her to give her hand so he could place air over the cut.

"I can do it myself. Wouldn't want to give you an STD."

Reece laughed loudly at her comment as he reached over the counter and grabbed her hand.

"For you, I'll take any STD."

Reece winked at her as he placed the Band-Aid and then pulled her hand up to his mouth and kissed her knuckles above the cut.

"All better now," he winked at her again.

"We'll just pretend that wasn't fucking weird and that chivalry isn't dead."

Reece laughed wholeheartedly at her joke, and he could see her face softening as the corners of her mouth perked up into a smile. "

If it would make you feel better, he wasn't wrong about how great your pussy is."

Crissie reached over and lightly smacked him with the back of her hand. "Don't mock me."

A small smile played on her lips as she took another swig of the bottle, holding it out to him. Reece took a big gulp of the bottle, feeling the familiar warmth down his throat.

"Luckily, my shift is almost done, and I can go home."

Reece raised a brow at her. "No, you still need to give me a lesson."

Crissie ran her hand through her hair. "This week just keeps getting better and better."

Reece looked at her and noted the extreme frustration on her face. As much as he wanted to believe her frustration was because of him, he could tell there was a lot more on her mind. "What do you mean?"

Crissie sighed loudly as she took the bottle back from him and swallowed two more mouthfuls. "Everything is going to shit." Crissie took another swig as he stared at her intently, waiting for her to continue.

"Firstly, my return to the bar was met by the news that sales are declining and therefore I can't pay my mortgage that is 4 months behind. So the bank might repossess my house that was built by my dead father. To top it off, my piece of shit car decided to die, so it's at a mechanic that I can't pay. I'm reduced to walking."

Crissie took another swig of the Bourbon. "And the

absolute best part of it all is that my side gig, the motorcycle lessons, is not working out because only one person signed up. It just so happens to be a guy I slept with years ago."

"Wait, you own this bar?" Reece looked around for a moment, taking in the entire space.

Crissie nodded, "I co-own it with Alex, the guy that signed you in for the lessons."

Crissie kept her eyes pinned on Reece. For the first time the entire morning, she noticed the wealth oozing off of him. Everything about him screamed power and money, from the designer Diesel Jeans to the brand new, top-of-the-line iPhone on the counter.

Subconsciously, her hand went towards her back pocket that held her cracked iPhone 6. She suddenly felt embarrassed to be complaining about her money troubles when it clearly wasn't something that he struggled with at all.

"It's rather an impressive establishment. Also explains why you can threaten customers and not get fired." Reece chuckled as he watched her expression intently.

"Sorry for unpacking all of my issues and that you had to see that. I can't tolerate men that have no manners."

Reece laughed again, and her embarrassment deepened.

"Don't feel embarrassed. It was bad-ass, and I don't mind you unpacking at all."

Crissie felt even worse now. "I will do your lessons as one last hoorah before I have to close down the bar forever."

Reece frowned deeply. "Closing down?"

Crissie sighs again, handing him the bottle. "I will probably sell this place and use the money to save my house and fix my car."

Reece looked at her confused and then gave the place another once over, his plan becoming clearer and more transparent.

"How does your business partner feel about all of that?" Reece questions, taking a swig of the bottle and handing it back to Crissie.

"It was his idea, actually. He knows it'll be the easiest way to get me out of my financial problem.

Crissie swigs from the bottle again, the agitation of her situation dawning on her again.

Reece stares into her eyes as the final pieces of his plan fall into place. "In that case, I might just have the perfect solution for you."

9

HER SAVING GRACE

"Wait, what? Repeat that one more time?"

Reece laughed at the perplexed expression on Crissie's face.

"It's simple. You offer up one week of your life. This week, you will teach me how to ride a motorcycle while completing the trip to The Olive Canyon Inn. After we return back here, we will part ways, and I will pay off your mortgage and pay the repairs to your car."

The deal sounded so unbelievable and mouth-watering, not that Crissie would ever admit it out loud.

"I am not a charity case Reece," Crissie said it softly. But the way his name rolled off her tongue set him on fire. She feared he was getting the wrong impression of her.

"I am not saying you are. I want to take the trip, and I want you to take it with me. I am purely paying you for your time."

This set her off even more. "That makes me sound like whore."

Reece stared at her again, and she felt unbelievably small under his intense gaze.

"That is not my intention. I am simply paying you for the lesson and bike ride. If you want to ride me, you'll have to do so at your own cost."

He tried his level best to convince her without offending her, but it felt like he was saying all of the wrong things.

Reece had been closing business deals since he was 16. Yet, somehow, this negotiation was a hell of a lot harder than any meeting he had to complete. Crissie didn't look convinced at all.

"Just think about it. You have nothing to lose besides your time."

Crissie knew that wasn't true. She could lose her dignity, self-control, and possibly some of her self-worth too. She wasn't fooling herself to believe that she wasn't attracted to him. In fact, the more she looked at him, the more she wanted to spend another night with him. The simple fact of the matter was that she would probably end up sleeping with him or, worse, falling in love with him.

"What are you so afraid of?" he stated once he saw how much the wheels in her head were turning.

Crissie didn't answer him. There was a lot to be afraid of. He offered enough to be scared of. That was her biggest fear, accidentally falling in love with him and having her heartbroken.

"I will think about it, I promise."

Reece was the skeptical one now. He wasn't about to force her into a situation she wasn't comfortable with.

"Take two days to mull it over, sleep on it, and then we'll talk again. If in two days you're not up for it, we don't do it," and just like that, he handed her the ball back. It was in her court now, and the decision was hers and hers alone.

Reece swallowed the last of the Bourbon and gave her a 100 dollar bill. His intentions were not to make her feel intimidated by his money. Still, he wanted to pay for both his cocktail and the Bourbon they drank together.

As he left the bar, he could feel Crissie's gaze on his ass, and, for a moment, he felt thankful that he spent so much time squatting at the gym.

As he got in his car, he noticed the sign in front of the parking spot. It read Reserved for Cristina Fox in massive bold letters. Suddenly her frustration about the parking spot made sense, and he chuckled to himself. He'd been getting under her skin even before he introduced himself that morning.

Reece drove straight back to his suite and ordered a steak dinner. The alcohol was gnawing at his stomach in a way he hadn't known since his university days. After his dinner, Reece sat and thought about Alexis once more, hoping that she would agree to their little trip with every inch of his being.

Crissie walked home, despite having enough tips to get a cab. She preferred the walk and hoped it would clear her head and give her the answers she so desperately needed. It wasn't an easy choice to make, and she knew full well that she'd always regret it if she said no.

Her walk did absolutely nothing to help her reach a decision. Her mind still seemed like a battlefield, and she was all over the place. Crissie knew she had to clear her mind, so she decided to clean up her act for the first time in months.

Crissie had always been the type of person that had everything in order. Her house was always spotless, and everything had a place, but since her break-up, she lacked the motivation to do anything but drown her sorrows in cheap wine and ice cream. However, unknowingly, she had decided to forgive and forget everything that her ex had done to her.

Crissie didn't know what to do about the trip but, as she started cleaning up her entire house. She slowly began to let go of all the pain, rage, and frustration that had built up since her trip to the flower shop. Even though she had felt no pain or issues when she saw the woman that stole her man, Crissie had unknowingly held on to a tiny sliver of hope that he would magically return to her.

All of her flirting with Reece had given her the groove back that she lost. For the first time in many years, she felt like herself again. As she washed away the years of memories she created with her ex, she felt lighter and happier.

In her pursuit of a new beginning, Crissie came across the last items that tied her to her ex-fiancé. As she stuffed all of those items of clothing, jewelry, and stuffed animals into a garbage bag, she purged him from her life. When the entire house was clean and everything was back to how Crissie loved it, it was well past midnight.

Crissie stepped back and took a look around. The place finally looked like hers again. Crissie was more than happy with the way everything had turned out, and with all of her things back in their rightful places, Crissie was finally ready to go to bed. That night Crissie got in her bed, and her heart soul felt lighter, and she felt free. So she slept like a rock.

10

DISTRACTIONS

I t had been nearly a day since he had agreed to give Crissie time to decide, but Reece was slowly spiraling. Thoughts of her consumed his mind, and he found himself periodically checking the phone to see if she had called or left a message that he might have missed. This feeling was strange to Reece and, in all of his years of dating; he'd never experienced the borderline-stalking that he felt right now.

Reece had always been the type of person to think twice and act once. Still, when it came to a certain Cristina Fox, he was reduced to nothing more than a teenager going through puberty. Reece had tried just about every avenue he could think of to get rid of the physical problem she created.

Much to his dismay, he even tried watching pornography. But even then, he found himself constantly looking for a woman that resembled her beauty. When he came up empty-handed, he reverted back to his own perverted fantasies. That is precisely where he found himself now; rock hard despite the cold water that flowed over him in the shower.

Still plagued by the memories of that night years ago, Reece gripped his shaft and slowly started moving his hand up and down. Ever so slightly running his thumb across the head each time his palm came close to it. In his mind, he clearly envisioned Crissie on her knees, one hand stroking the shaft as she bobbed up and down, taking him as far down her throat as she could. He could practically feel each movement as she swirled her tongue over the tip and played with his balls.

It didn't take long for him to spray a thick stream of cum over the shower wall and, as he rinsed the evidence of his escapade off the walls and himself, he didn't feel any better. Reece stepped out of the shower and rechecked his phone, making sure that he had not missed her call. But once again, he came up empty-handed.

Across town, Crissie had taken a much different approach to distract herself from the pending decision. Instead, she decided that it was time to consult the advice of the one person that had been there for her through every single hard cross-road in her life.

An intense nervousness had taken place in her as she dialed her mother's number. She had no idea how she would even begin to explain the shit show that had become her life in the last 24 hours. After the third ring, somebody answered the phone, but it was not her mother's voice.

"Hello mommy," instead of being greeted by her mother, Zoe spoke into the phone.

"Hello, my love," Crissie greeted, "what are you doing?"

The little girl giggled softly. "Nana went to take a nap, so I'm watching YouTube." Crissie couldn't hide the smile on her face and much less the tears that bloomed in her eyes.

"That's nice, my love. How was school?"

Crissie listened intently as her daughter relayed her

entire day. Zoe jumped from one topic to another, and the more she spoke, the closer Crissie got to tears.

"Oh, and mommy, I watched a movie today. And we ate dino nuggies. It was delicious."

Crissie smiled as the first tear ran down her cheek. "What movie did you watch, my love?"

Zoe was quiet for a bit. "It had all of these little people, and it had a pink elephant and these bubble gums, I think. And there was a train, it was really good, but Nana said it was dark. I don't know why because the lights were on."

Crissie chuckled at the little girl's explanation. "It sounds like a good movie."

Crissie kept listening to her daughter rambling about her dolls and toys. Eventually, she heard her mother calling Zoe in the background.

"Bye, mommy, I love you!" and with that, the girl handed the phone to her Nana.

"Hi Crissie, is everything all right?" as her mother spoke, her tears flowed freely.

"Yes, mom, I'm going to bed. I love you."

Her mother said her goodbyes, and Crissie felt the tears worsen. And in that state, she cried herself to sleep.

CRISSIE WOKE up the following day, and she had already decided. Crissie knew it was time to face the music and let Reece know what she had decided on. She knew this decision would make or break her, and she was finally okay with that.

Reece was intensely busy in the gym when he heard his phone ringing halfway through his set. He finally gave in and answered the call even though his mind taunted him constantly because he was religiously checking if she'd called yet.

"Hunter," his greeting was very gruff and annoyed.

For a moment, Crissie desperately wanted to back out of whatever she was about to say. "That's a shitty way to answer the phone."

When he heard her voice, he almost dropped the phone out of surprise. "Crissie?" His voice came out a lot more surprised than he intended, and he heard her laugh on the other end.

"Yes, don't act so surprised. You gave me your number and told me to call, remember?"

There was playfulness in her voice, and that broke all of the tension in his bones. "I do. I just doubted you'd call, that's all."

Crissie sat cross-legged on her bathroom floor, playing with the piece of paper he'd written his number on. She understood his point because she also doubted whether she'd call.

"I'll do the trip," her reply was lightning fast, and if Reece wasn't paying such close attention, he'd have missed it completely.

"That's great..."

"But, I have some ground rules, okay?" She cut him off.

Reece loved how bossy she could get. "Ground rules?"

Crissie cleared her throat. "One: I will only be teaching you how to ride, nothing more and nothing less. Second: We will not sleep together under any circumstances, understood?"

Despite Reece feeling like they would definitely be sleeping together on this trip, he agreed to her demands. They set a time to meet up and drive to the Olive Canyon Inn. Reece was excited for the prospect of what could happen, not just because he might get to have her in his bed again. No, he was excited because he would get to spend time with her. Reece was beginning to enjoy time with Crissie purely because of how great her personality was. He always had a smile when he was around her, and that was a far cry from his normal day-to-day life.

11

ROAD TRIP FUN

C rissie stood at the entrance to the bar and waited rather impatiently for Reece to arrive. As time ticked on, her anxiety grew worse, and she started doubting herself and her choice to go with him on the trip. Crissie knew that it was too late to back out now, and, despite how badly she wanted to, she couldn't convince herself that the trip would turn out okay.

It had been two days since she agreed, and in those two days, she'd debated with herself heavily about her decision. Crissie didn't even have the guts to tell her mother the real reason why she was embarking on this trip and instead opted to only tell her she'd be out of town for a week. In a way, Crissie wanted to keep Reece her secret for as long as possible. Even though she made him promise to not sleep with her, she knew full well that it would most probably happen.

Crissie was not opposed to the idea at all, and every time she heard his voice, she was just about ready to kick her shoes under his bed and spend the night. She had decided to be rather smart on the trip. Because they'd be spending a lot of time together, she thought it reasonable to pack her trusty vibrator in case the temptation became too great.

As Crissie stood, she checked the time only to realize that Reece was almost fifteen minutes late. With her phone in hand, she was just about to call him when an SUV pulled into the parking lot and came to a halt in front of her.

Reece got out and took her bag. As he moved towards the trunk, she admired each muscle as they moved, following him with her eyes until he closed the trunk.

"If you continue eye-fucking me, we'll break your rules before we even reach the end of town."

Crissie scoffed loudly, "I was not. I was actually trying to figure out if blue was your color, and it turns out it's not."

Crissie walked around to the passenger door and realized that he was not driving an SUV, and instead, it was a brand-new Jeep. Crissie tried to not show how much his scent overwhelmed her when she shut the door; so instead, she turned on the radio and found a station that played classic rock.

Reece stared at her as she toyed with the controls to the radio. It surprised him that she was so comfortable in his car. "You look great today."

Crissie looked at him, "I thought we agreed that we wouldn't sleep together?"

Reece took his eyes off the road for a second and stared into hers, "it was an innocent compliment. I could have said you look edible in those jeans if that is better suited?"

Crissie rolled her eyes, "it's not, but thank you."

They drove in silence for a while until Crissie spotted a restaurant and garage station up ahead.

"Stop here. I want a bacon burger and cheesy jalapeno fries."

This surprised him even more, but he happily obliged her request and pulled into the roadhouse parking lot.

"Hello. One combo number 7. An order of Mexican corn fritters and a kiwi-strawberry lemonade, please," Crissie ordered directly to the teenage boy that waited patiently and wrote down the order once she finished.

She turned to Reece, "Oh, do you want anything?"

He thought for a second, "I'll have the same," the boy relayed their order back to them and gave them the total.

Reece pulled out his bank card and handed it to the waiter before Crissie even had the chance. As the boy took hold of the card, his eyes went wide. Reece didn't seem to even notice the reaction as he went about filling out the slip and signing for the food. The boy handed back the card. As Reece put it back in his wallet, Crissie caught a glimpse of the black metal.

At that moment, Crissie wished she had declined the trip. Seeing his black American Express card made it very clear that they were in two very different leagues. He wasn't just rich. Reece Hunter was mega-rich, and that set fear into her veins. What was she thinking fucking around with a man like him?

It had been around 10 minutes since Reece paid for the food, and Crissie was panicking more than ever. Usually, a man with his type of money would never look twice at her, and yet, he insisted she come on this trip.

"Where did you grow up?" Crissie needed something to stop the absolute panic that ran rampant in her brain. Unfortunately, that was the first question that she came up with.

"New York, you?" Reece took the food from the waiter and gave one bag and drink over to Crissie.

"Texas, thank you for the food." Despite her rampant

thoughts, Crissie dived right into her fries, not even sparing one glance at Reece.

Reece ate while staring at Crissie. He was amazed how a woman could be so comfortable in his presence. Reece had purposefully paid with his black Amex card. He always did that when he did something with women he was interested in, purely because their reactions could tell you a lot about their character.

Like every aspect he got to learn about her, Crissie was different when she saw it. He had seen the panic that set in clear as day. He didn't understand why she got so worried about the card. Still, he was thankful that she didn't start an entire conversation based solely on how he made money or how much he actually had in the bank.

"Did you enjoy growing up in New York?" The pair had finished their food, and Reece was pleasantly surprised with the taste.

"As much as a kid can in the concrete jungle. I spent more time in boardrooms and school than I did being a kid. What was Texas like growing up?"

Crissie smiled brightly, "I had a completely different childhood, to be honest. I spent most of my time climbing trees and playing ding dong ditch with the neighborhood kids."

This brought a small smile to Reece's face, "I've actually never played that before."

Crissie looked at him, completely dumbstruck. "Really?"

Reece nodded slowly. "My dad felt it was a waste of time, so I've never done it. Instead, I learned politics and foreign languages."

Crissie stared at him a few minutes more, and as they pulled into the Olive Canyon Inn, she mumbled quietly, "holy shit, your childhood sucked."

Reece laughed at her comment as they made their way into the reception area.

"Welcome to the Olive Canyon Inn. Do you have a reservation?"

Before Crissie could get a word in, Reece answered the lady behind the desk. "Yes, reservation is under Hunter."

The lady typed on her computer for a few seconds and then slid two keycards over to them. "Enjoy your stay."

As they turned around to walk away, the woman called Reece back. "For when the lady inevitably gets boring." With that, she slid the paper over to him and gave Crissie a dirty look.

Reece looked between the two women and slowly slid the paper back across the desk, "I'm good." With that, Reece walked past Crissie and out of the door, ready to get to his suite.

The walk to their suites was short, and Crissie was starting to feel the effect of the day on her body. At this stage in time, the only thing she wanted was a good night's rest.

"I got two suites, but if you want, you could always stay in mine tonight." Reece's voice was playful and teasing as he held out the two keycards.

"I thought we agreed, we won't be sleeping together?" Crissie felt like she'd been saying this a lot over the last couple of hours, but Reece just kept a coy smile on his face.

"Who said anything about sleeping?"

Crissie chuckled and ran her hand through her hair, taking one keycard from his hand. She opened the door to her suite. "Goodnight, Reece."

Crissie spent the night tossing and turning in bed. In all of her dreams, Reece made an appearance and, by the time morning rolled around, Crissie was more frustrated than she could ever have anticipated. The only thing on her mind was Reece, and she yearned to feel his touch, to feel the relief she knew he could bring.

There were only a few hours left before she had to meet him for breakfast and his first lesson. That was more than enough time to get the job done herself. Crissie rummaged between her clothes until she found her pink rabbit vibrator, and she set off on pleasuring herself. Crissie tried all positions and routes, but she came up empty-handed no matter how much she tried. At that moment, she knew that she was most definitely going to break her own rule.

12

LESSONS LEARNED

Reece stared intently at the way Crissie sat on the motorcycle. She was explaining the concepts to him, but all he could focus on was the way her legs wrapped around the seat. It hadn't even been two days, and already the tension between them was palpable. Reece didn't have a clue how he'd be keeping his hands off her for the rest of the week.

Crissie was beginning to see that riding a motorcycle was pure muscle memory. Reece had plenty of memories about riding. She didn't know whether those memories were about riding her or the bike, though. It didn't take a genius to figure out either way. He was paying absolutely no attention to what she was saying.

Crissie was to blame, and she knew it, but, in her defense, the weather had taken a turn, and the daisy dukes she was wearing were purely for her comfort and not his benefit. Crissie wanted so badly to believe that was the only reason, but she couldn't deny that she loved having his eyes on her and only her.

The two of them stood in the parking lot of The Olive

Canyon Inn. Crissie had tried to explain how the motorcycle worked to him to no avail. Now they were merely staring at the bike.

"Personally, I think you should just show me how to ride," the teasing smile was back on his face, and Crissie had a pretty good idea where things were headed.

Crissie got on the bike once more. "Make sure it's in neutral." She pointed to a lever just underneath the throttle. "Then turn the ignition key. Once you feel the bike pull away, put it in first gear, and pull the throttle until the bike is moving. Now just lift up your feet and cruise." She demonstrated the movement and slowly made a circle around him; stopping back in the same spot she started the demonstration.

Crissie got off the motorcycle and gave him the keys, motioning back to the bike. "Now you try."

Reece was reluctant, to say the least. He hadn't been on a bike in so many years, and the absolute last thing he wanted was to accidentally fall in front of Crissie. It was a strange thought to him. He'd never been the type to fear a bit of embarrassment, but here he was frankly terrified of it.

It didn't take long for him to actually mount the bike, purely because the only thing he feared more than falling was having Crissie think he was afraid. At that moment, it also became clear to him how much power this woman already possessed over him.

"Like this?" Reece put the bike in neutral, and when he went to start it, nothing happened at all.

"You have it in first gear."

Reece was about to argue with her. After all, she had stood back so far. There was no possible way she could see where he had the gears. Reece fiddled with the gears and tried again, and magically it started. He only got a few feet before the bike died again.

"No, do this," Crissie showed him something on the handlebars, but he was not paying attention to that. Instead, his eyes were drawn directly to the way her tank top moved as she bent forward.

"Nice bra," he commented.

The black lace that he could see filled his head with a lot of dirty ideas. The main one entailed bending her over the bike then and there and fucking her hard, in front of anybody that wanted to see. It took a lot of restraint for both of them to move on from the comment.

"Focus on the bike, not me."

Reece leaned down and let his breath fall over her neck. "How can I do that if I'd much rather prefer you ride me?"

Crissie's breath got caught in her throat. She normally had a lot to say. Her mind always conjured up a sarcastic remark in half of these situations, but with Reece, everything was different. She was different. For the umpteenth time that day, Crissie ignored the comment and instead focused on the task at hand. She only needed to get through five more lessons, and then she could go back to her dull and everyday life.

Crissie showed him the controls once again, subconsciously leaning more on him this time.

"Let's stop for today and go have dinner. We've been at this for hours."

This time it was Crissie that had a smirk plastered over her features. "You're trying to tell me you can't last a few hours."

Reece looked at her and shook his head. She sure knew how to get him hot and heavy.

Crissie got on the bike and drove it into a parking spot

close to the building. The bikes were a major part of Aunt Layla's income, and she wouldn't be too pleased if Crissie lost or damaged one.

The two of them walked in absolute silence back to their suites, occasionally brushing their hands against each other. Crissie was overthinking again. Her mind convinced her that she should not go any further than her door. But her body craved his touch once more.

Crissie couldn't think clearly, not that she had been at all since he walked into her life a week ago. But, as they came up to the doors of their rooms, Crissie couldn't decide just what she wanted.

"I really want to kiss you." Reece's voice was so serene and innocent as he confessed his thoughts, making it clear to Crissie that she wasn't the only one with these feelings.

Crissie wrapped her arms around his neck in a split-second decision and kissed him passionately, thoroughly, and fully. The kiss was something Crissie had never experienced before. A feeling of lightning coursed through her veins and made everything but the two of them disappear for a good while.

Reece placed his hands on her waist, deepening the kiss and exploring every inch of her mouth. The two of them stood, pressed up against the hallway in between the doors to their suites. Crissie broke their kiss for a second to unlock the door and pull him inside. They were both breathing heavily, but primal instinct was at play. With needy hands, they explored each other's bodies, running their hands over each other until they reached the bed.

Reece laid Crissie down on the soft covers and hovered over her for a second.

"So fucking beautiful."

As he whispered the words, goose bumps erupted all

over her flesh, but Reece was not wasting any time. He kissed a trail down from behind her ear until he reached her collarbone, and the material stopped him. It didn't take very long for him to rip off her shirt as she unclasped her bra and flung it across the room.

Reece didn't waste any time and placed his hands on her breasts, squeezing them as he played with the nipples. Bending down, he placed one kiss on her throat, working his way until he reached her nipples. Playfully, he bit it before softly licking it to soothe the sting.

Crissie found herself moaning his name softly as he trailed kisses down her stomach and above her pubic bone.

"You sure about this?" Reece had his thumbs hooked into the belt loops of her daisy dukes, but he stared at her and patiently waited for her answer.

She nodded slowly. "One hundred percent."

Reece pulled down her shorts and underwear, standing up for a moment and admiring the absolute beauty of Crissie as she laid on her back, squirming and begging for his attention. Reece kissed her inner thighs, stopping every so often to blow lightly over her core.

"Fuck, just do something already!"

Crissie was getting anxious. The anticipation was killing her as he took his sweet time. Reece moved closer to her core. The vibration of his chuckle caused Crissie to grab his head and connect it with her pussy. She wanted nothing more than to feel him, to feel anything that would bring her relief as he teased her.

Reece tried restraint as he slowly licked up her slit, but that idea went completely out of the window as he got the first taste of her sweet juices. With intense fervor, he circled her clit, moving up and down to taste more of her. As he worked his way up and down her most intimate parts, he couldn't get enough.

Slowly he inserted one finger into her, moving in and out as he continued to eat her out like she had never been. Crissie's breathing became erratic as she swore lightly, curling her back up and away from the bed. Reece picked up his pace, even more, inserting another finger and then another. Leisurely, he bent his finger upwards as he thrust them in, grazing her G-spot as he did. It didn't take long for Crissie to scream out his name, holding his head against her as she fell from the cliff and into the abyss.

Crissie had never come by oral sex before, and she was hell bent on saying thank you as he removed his fingers from her and licked them clean. With shaky legs, Crissie pulled him down, so he laid on the bed, she straddled him, and in one swift movement, she took all of him inside of her.

Crissie could feel how he filled her perfectly. With every upwards motion, she felt alive. Crissie swore softly as he grabbed ahold of her hips, pushing into her with intense passion. Reece could not believe the view that had been bestowed on him. For his position beneath her, he could see every curve of her body. He could hear every moan and hiss as he moved inside of her. Reece felt incredibly lucky to be there in the moment as Crissie bounced up and down on top of him.

Reece dug his fingers into her hips as she clamped down on him. He was so close to coming that he didn't know how long he'd be able to hold it back anymore. Reece kept thrusting, and as soon as he felt Crissie unwind, he did too, shooting thick ropes of his cum into the condom.

Afterward, the two of them just laid there in each other's embrace for a while. Crissie couldn't believe how satisfying it was to be with a man that pushed you over the edge and into oblivion.

"Shower?"

Reece couldn't help but stare at her perfect breasts as she spoke. He nodded once, not even sure what the question had been. Crissie pulled him up by his hand and dragged him into the bathroom.

Reece stood behind Crissie as the water rolled down the both of them. The steam clouded his vision as he rubbed berry scented body wash all over her, making sure to wash away all of his evidence from her body. Crissie relished in the feeling of his hands on her body as he took his time to diligently wash her.

As Crissie leaned back, she felt his fully erected excitement push into her lower back, the erotic nature of their shower evident on his body.

13

CAR RIDES AND CONVERSATIONS

I n the restaurant, they sat opposite each other. Crissie had changed into a red summer dress, and Reece couldn't keep his eyes off her.

"You look gorgeous," he remarked as she reached for her glass of wine.

Crissie smiled at him, and he could feel his heart beating faster. He felt like a teenager on a first date when, in reality, they were two adults that barely knew each other, and they weren't even close to being on a date.

The incredible sex they had a few nights ago was still playing on his mind, and he was sure Crissie felt the same way. He wanted desperately to have her again, to taste her, and to feel her warmth envelop him as he thrust into her with devilish intensity. He wasn't expecting her to do anything again, and he was content with the two nights she'd already given him. And deep down, he knew that regardless of it all, she'd set the bar very high for every other woman that he'd spend the night with.

"Why choose this place for a vacay?" Crissie had wanted to ask since he stepped into the bar that fateful day. A man with his type of money could go just about anywhere in the world, and yet he decided on a place in the middle of nowhere.

"It's peaceful and quiet. Honestly, it's the only place I can ever come to just escape it all." And because I had hoped to meet somebody like you, he desperately wanted to add but decided not to.

"I hated spending summers in Texas when I was a kid. Everybody would go to Los Angeles or New York, and I'd be stuck here."

Crissie had resorted to small talk or, well, anything that would calm her raging hormones. Reece had insisted that they have dinner at one of the fancier restaurants at the Olive Canyon Inn and had she known he'd wear a button-up and slacks. She'd insisted they go to McDonald's.

Reece looked absolutely divine in his formal wear. The actual trademark of a businessman with power, and no matter how hard she tried, her mind only wanted one thing tonight. And it was most definitely not on the fancy printed menu.

"New York isn't that great either."

Crissie found that extremely hard to believe. She always wanted to visit but never had the opportunity or cash. "Why?" she asked.

"I never got to see the greatness of it. I went from the womb to work. And that made me into what I am today, so I can't complain too much."

Crissie ate some of her steak as he spoke. Despite the price of the steak, it was absolutely perfect.

"What work do you do?" Crissie loved hearing Reece speak about his work. It gave her an intense amount of joy to see his eyes light up as he spoke.

"I own a business rescue company. If a company starts to

deteriorate or go bankrupt, I buy it and essentially save it from closing down."

A lot made sense to Crissie at that point. That's why he was paying for her lessons for a week. It was in his nature to want to save businesses, and that's precisely what he was doing for the bar.

She was worried that he would start thinking she was easy because she gave in to his temptation so quickly, but it all made sense now. Why would he give any thoughts to a biker chick that owned a nondescript bar in an obscure area in the middle of nowhere, Texas? Although the knowledge should've made her angry or even apprehensive about flirting with him, Crissie felt that it set her free.

If this was all a game to Reece, she could take his words to heart and a week from now, she'd be out of financial trouble, and Zoe could move back in with her. A part of her did feel sad because she'd come to really enjoy his company. But, truth be told, she had a feeling that this wouldn't go any further than just casual hooking up from the start.

The pair chatted about a lot of things throughout their dinner.

"Do you travel often?" Crissie asked as dessert was being served.

"Somewhat, I work quite a lot, so when I have the opportunity, I like to travel and do all of the things I missed out on during university. Do you?"

Crissie shook her head. "Not outside of Texas."

Reece kept his eyes pinned to her as she ate her cheesecake.

"Would you like some?"

Her question was innocent, and she was more than willing to split her portion and place half on his plate. However, Reece saw this as an open invitation. Sliding across the side of the booth, he moved into place right next to her. As she swallowed her bite, he planted his lips firmly on hers.

Reece touched his tongue to her lips, asking for permission to explore her mouth, and Crissie granted him access without a second thought. Just like their kiss in the hallway, this kiss was full of need and instinct. As they kissed, Crissie could feel his hand inching higher on her thigh, his fingers playing with the hemline.

"The cheesecake isn't sweet enough," Reece whispered in her ear before rejoining their lips.

Neither of them had any care in the world as her hands laid on his chest. Crissie opened her legs a tiny bit to give him more access, and Reece took it without hesitation.

Within seconds he had her underwear pushed to the side, his finger playing with her clit and wetness. Crissie completely forgot about the people around them and let out a soft moan.

"Quiet now, I wouldn't want the entire restaurant to see my dessert."

Crissie tried to keep quiet, but she danced so close to the edge. She knew that she'd come at any moment and that it would be everything but quiet.

Just before she reached her breaking point, she felt Reece withdraw his fingers from her body. The pair made intense eye contact as he licked his fingers clean.

"Now that's how I like my dessert."

Crissie's eyes were wide as everything that just happened dawned on her. Instead of feeling embarrassed, she was horny, and she needed Reece more than she had ever wanted anybody else.

Crissie motioned to the waiter. She needed to get the check and get out of here before she decided to fuck Reece in front of the entire restaurant. Reece seemed to read her mind and rushed the payment process along. Both Crissie and Reece sped to the car, eager to start the trip back to either one of their suites.

The moment they set foot in the car, Crissie realized she didn't even need to wait until they reached the suite. Reece was focused only on one thing, getting to the suite before he couldn't take it anymore. He had just pulled out of the parking lot when he felt cold hands undoing his belt buckle and pants.

Crissie was in a weird position with the gear shift poking into her side, but she couldn't care less at that moment. As soon as she moved his boxers out of the way, his cock sprang to life and stood at attention right in front of her eyes. Crissie grabbed his shaft and began stroking lightly as she ran her tongue from the tip all the way to the base. Crissie closed her eyes and bobbed on the head before taking the entire length down her throat.

As she cleared her gag reflex, Crissie applied a bit of pressure, and she could hear Reece swearing, his knuckles white as he gripped the steering wheel and tried to not let the car swerve at all. Crissie moved her head back up and looked him in the eyes as she stroked him with her right hand. Being so close to him, she could smell his cologne incredibly well. The smell alone made her wetter and needier than she could handle.

Crissie continued to bob up and down his cock, continuously stroking him until she felt him tense up. Suddenly she released him from her mouth, allowing him to stay rock hard as she took his balls in her mouth. She applied minimal pressure as she continued to stroke him, swirling his balls in her mouth ever so slightly.

Reece was beside himself with want, and the need for

her was stronger than he had ever experienced before. Crissie released his balls and deep throated him again. This time she allowed him to come, swallowing every last drop as he blew down her throat. When he was done, Crissie continued to bob on his cock, and when she came up, Reece couldn't wait anymore.

About a mile away from their suites, he pulled over, stopping the car completely on the side of the road. He didn't need to ask or convince Crissie because, by the time he switched off the ignition, she had already removed her underwear.

Crissie straddled him a few moments later, indulging in the sweet relief he brought as he stretched her core to accommodate his size. The car wasn't the most comfortable place to have sex, but neither cared as they moved slowly. This time around, everything was different. The sex wasn't hard and rough like the previous two times. Instead, it was slow and sensual as he kissed her tenderly while she moved up and down. Without either of them realizing it, this was the turning point.

14

THE WAY BACK

"When the fuck did that happen?"

Crissie was still half asleep when she heard Reece screaming into the phone. He wasn't loud per se, but it was apparent that there was some sort of problem.

She was still naked from the night before. As she started to untangle herself from the sheets, she couldn't help but feel incredibly grateful. Despite all of her fears and worries, the week had gone down smoothly. Crissie was also very thankful that Reece had satisfied her in a way that nobody had been able to. Crissie dropped the sheets on the ground as she made her way towards the bathroom, a part of her wished that Reece would turn around and join her, but he was much too busy with the conversation at hand.

"What do we do now?" Reece waited for his father to speak, but the old man was unusually quiet. When he came on this trip, everything had been going great, the Dubai deal had gone through, and the stocks were recovering. The week had been one of the best he'd ever had, and now it was all going to shit.

"I don't know, son. We have to wait it out and hope it isn't going to ruin us."

The statement was not calming him down in the slightest. He knew that he had to get back to work as soon as possible, and that was a far cry from the thought he had just moments before the phone call fucked it all up.

Reece said his goodbyes and hung up the phone. The environment was peaceful and quiet as he sat on the balcony and stared out over the river. He could hear the shower running and Crissie as she hummed softly. His first instinct was to join her, to enjoy one last moment of pure bliss with her before he had to return to his busy life all the way back in New York. As he sat there, he realized that he would miss the things he had with Crissie and, for the first time in his life, it was a deeper connection than just the physical intimacy they shared.

Reece was very shocked at his realization. Quite frankly, he was downright terrified of what it actually meant. He'd never been the commitment or white picket fence type, but he realized what his life lacked when he was with Crissie. Reece didn't know what to do with the newfound feelings he had discovered, but he was well aware that he needed to decide really fast.

Crissie got out of the shower and dressed comfortably. She was more than a little sore, and it didn't take a genius to know it was because Reece was much more gifted than anybody else she'd been within the last few years. Crissie looked herself in the mirror, and for the first time since her breakup almost 10 months ago, her reflection was happy and healthy.

Crissie couldn't wait to get back home so she could see her daughter. And now that her financial problems were at an end, she could finally have Zoe with her again. Crissie stared at herself again for a moment, relieved that she was finally returning back to her old self.

"Good morning," she exclaimed as she walked into the open area of the suite.

Reece seemed distant and quiet. "Good morning to you too." His voice was playful and teasing, but Crissie could tell his heart wasn't in it.

They packed their bag and loaded them into the car, both of them stoic and silent. Crissie was more than a little confused by how Reece was acting towards her, but she chalked it up to the phone call he had while she was in the shower.

"When are you headed back?" They were more than halfway back to town now, and Crissie couldn't stand the awkward silence anymore.

"Later today," he replied, his eyes still pinned to the road. "There are problems at the office, and I'm needed urgently."

Crissie didn't know why it bothered her so much. They both had agreed to split ways after the trip. He'd go back to his fancy New York apartment, and she'd pay off her house and fix her car.

Crissie had the hope that maybe; just maybe, Reece would change his mind and want to stay with her. Now it was a hard pill to swallow because he was going to give her up that easily. As they entered the town and she directed Reece to her house, Crissie found herself unnecessarily anxious about what would happen once they arrived. Fantasies played on a loop in her mind, but Reece stopped all of it as they stopped.

They parked in her driveway and got out. Reece

removed her bag from the trunk and placed it on the paving next to her.

"Goodbye Crissie, I hope we meet again in the future."

After asking for her banking details, he got back in the car and drove out of her life. Crissie was emotional, and she hated the fact that he had now left her twice with nothing more than fleeting memories.

Crissie knew she needed to do something to keep herself from crying, and that's exactly what she did the moment she stepped foot into the house.

"Hi mom, is Zoe there?" Crissie couldn't wait to hear her daughter's voice, but instead of hearing the chirpy voice of her five-year-old, her mother let out a loud sigh.

"I tried calling earlier, but your phone went to voicemail."

Crissie could hear the worry in her mother's tone. "The signal was bad on the road. Mom. What's going on?"

There was another long pause from her mother. "Zoe caught a cold. The doctor feared it might turn into pneumonia, so he admitted her to the pediatric ward for observation."

Crissie felt her knees buckling as she dropped to the floor, "I... I'll be right there."

Crissie dialed a cab with shaking hands, and the moment she stepped foot into it, the dam broke, and her tears flowed freely. In the short cab ride, she cried for herself, for Reece that left, and most importantly, she cried for her daughter that had to be in the hospital without her mother by her side.

20,000 FEET ABOVE HER HEAD, sitting in the comfort of his private jet, Reece reprimanded himself for being such a coward. He knew that he would break her heart if he was so cold and cruel, but he felt like he had no choice in the matter simply because he was too scared to love any woman as fiercely as he was beginning to love her.

15

MONEY NIGHTMARES

C rissie arrived at the hospital only to find a smiling and bubbly Zoe sitting on the bed laughing loudly at something the nurse said.

"Mommy!" she shouted as she laid eyes on her mother.

Crissie felt herself release a breath she didn't know she was holding.

"Hi, I'm Cristina Fox, Zoe's mom."

The nurse smiles brightly. "I am Nurse Turner. Zoe, you were right. Your mommy is very pretty. We'll be right back, okay, sweetie?"

Zoe nods to the nurse as she turns her attention back to the coloring book in front of her.

"Zoe is a strong girl, and she's doing remarkable. She has a bit of an infection, so we prescribed some antibiotics to clear it right up. She is stable, but the doctor recommends we keep her here one more night just to be on the safe side. So you can take her home in the morning."

Crissie nods as the nurse speaks, relief washing over her as the nurse reassures her that Zoe will be okay.

Crissie lays in the hospital bed with Zoe by her side. For the first time since Reece dropped her off that morning, Crissie felt a sense of happiness. Crissie felt disappointed in herself for giving in so easily. She didn't regret the weekend of sex, but she did regret giving away her heart. Crissie was always a guarded person; it took her ex months to get this kind of loyalty, and yet, it only took Reece a week.

Crissie didn't even care about the money anymore. She just wanted Reece to be here with her. She wanted to wake up with him and to go to bed with him, and, most of all, she wanted the happiness he gave her. The thought didn't scare Crissie half as much as she was afraid it would. Instead, it filled her with a deep sense of sadness.

Crissie found herself staring at the ceiling of the hospital room, unable to sleep or think about anything other than Reece. Just shy of two a.m., Crissie decided to go about and find herself a midnight snack in the cafeteria. She said a silent prayer that her card would not be declined as she picked up the items.

In her mind, Crissie calculated the cost of her stuff to be under 16 dollars, and panic settled in her when she realized the cashier was swiping a transaction of over 20 dollars. Crissie stood paralyzed for a moment when the transaction went through. Rushing across the cafeteria, she entered the hospital room and searched for her phone in the dark.

Crissie waited impatiently for her online banking to load, and once she saw the total, she refreshed the page twice more. Her account balance was 125,000 dollars. A full $100,000 dollars more than she had agreed on with Reece. Crissie dialed his number without even thinking twice about it. She needed to thank him, and more importantly, she needed to know why he sent her so much money.

The phone rang for a few moments and then went to voicemail. With it, Crissie's heart sunk down towards her shoes. Crissie stared at the phone again, puzzled as she dialed, and this time it went straight to voicemail. Crissie hoped he was just busy and not ignoring her, and, for a moment, she regretted calling in the first place.

Crissie got back in the bed next to her daughter. The midnight snacks were long forgotten, and she tried to sleep. However, the only thing she could dream about was her nights spent entangled with Reece Hunter. But, even in those dreams, Reece did not want to be with her. Crissie woke up a few times during the night, each time in a cold sweat with her breath racing.

Crissie got up and checked her phone each time, but there was only silence as Reece ignored her texts. Crissie was beginning to feel intensely sad at the way things were playing out, and she wished Reece would just answer the phone so they could talk, even if it was just one last time.

Back in his high-rise New York office, Reece stared at the phone as it rang, too much of a coward to even answer it. Halfway through her call, he declined and, as soon as she called again, he declined as well. He felt disgusted with himself but, truth be told, Reece didn't know what to do or how to go about the intense feeling he was having. The only thing he did know was that he couldn't give her that much power over him, ever.

Reece had tried to get his mind off Crissie, but, just like the last time, he wasn't accomplishing much. He could still sense her at every turn he made. He felt like the ghost of her was hiding in the shadows and her scent lingered in his clothes. Reece was terrified of spending the rest of his life always looking in the shadows to see if he could catch a glimpse of her. As opposed to that, he was even more terrified to be with her and give her all of him.

Reece was under no impression that he was a whole man. He knew there were parts of him that had been broken a long time ago and, even if Crissie was the key to fixing them, he never wanted to be the person that caused her any pain or grief. Reece felt trapped between a rock and a hard place, a catch-22 that he had no idea how to solve.

Reece wanted so badly to reach out to her but, even then, he had no clue how to do it. So he did the only thing he knew how to do. He poured himself into his work. Diving in headfirst and hoping that it would help him forget about Texas, about Crissie, and most important, about her body that haunted his thoughts and dreams.

CRISSIE SIGNED the paperwork that guaranteed her daughter could go home and be back in her own space. After dropping both her mother and daughter home, she drove to the mortgage office.

The clerk looked surprised to see her. Not even two weeks ago, she was begging for an extension, and now she was paying off every last cent she owed in one transaction. The man wanted to comment about it, but he could see the pain and lack of sleep on Crissie's face. The moment the transaction went through, Crissie signed the paperwork and disappeared out of the front door.

Crissie had hoped that she'd feel lighter once she had paid it off, but she still felt like the weight of the world sat on her shoulders. The feeling was driving her insane, and she wanted nothing more than to go back to Reece's embrace, to just be with him and forget that everything else existed.

Crissie paid for the fixing of her car and drove all the way to the bar. She had secretly hoped that the Jeep would be in her parking spot, but it was empty, just like her heart. Crissie sat in her car in front of the bar for a long fifteen minutes. Trying to find the strength to go inside and face Alex and the clients. However, she felt worse than she did two weeks ago when she returned after everything in her life imploded the first time.

Crissie felt like she could kick her own ass. She had promised herself she wouldn't make the mistake of falling in love with Reece, and yet, that is precisely what she wound up doing. Crissie was furious at him for just upping and leaving like she meant absolutely nothing to him. Even more than that, she was angry at herself. She was mad that she gave her heart away so quickly, even when she promised herself she wouldn't do it ever again.

Crissie wanted nothing more than to just crawl into her bed and cry her woes away, but she couldn't stand the thought of another eight months spent crying over a man that didn't want her. Crissie wiped the stray tear that ran down her cheek and checked her reflection in the side-view mirror. With one smile, she felt confident that her mask was on securely and that nobody would be able to see the pain she was masking. With that, she stepped out of the car and made her way to the bar, praying to whatever deity above that nobody would realize she was dying inside.

Alex sensed something was wrong the moment Crissie stepped foot into the bar. He'd spoken to her a few times while she was on her trip with Mr. Hunter. As she made her way toward him, Alex could tell there wasn't the same spark in her that he could hear over the phone. Without question or regret, he poured her a hefty shot of tequila and handed it to her as she placed her stuff down behind the bar.

Crissie swallowed the liquor and gave him a hug. As Alex wrapped his arms around her, he could feel the tears escaping her eyes as they landed softly on his shirt.

"What's going on, spill. Now!" he whispered to her as she pulled away to wipe her tears away.

16

DARK CLOUDS DURING CELEBRATION

Alex was conflicted as he listened to Crissie recount the entire situation. On the one hand, he couldn't help but be happy that his best friend is finally free of her financial troubles; on the other hand, he was pissed at Reece for leaving her without closure.

Crissie was full-on crying as she finished the story. "And now I have $100K that I don't know what to do with."

To Alex, the answer seemed simple. "Buy a new car and then take Zoe to Disney World. It's that simple, you have the money now, just spend it."

Crissie shook her head furiously. "No, not until I know why he did me such a favor. He could've just made a mistake and wants it back."

Both of them knew Crissie was just spiraling.

"He has a black Amex. I highly doubt he's going to miss the money. Hell, there is probably more than that in change over at his house."

Crissie laughed at his joke, her tears starting to come to a halt. She wasn't convinced, though. She felt like there had to be an ulterior motive to his generosity. Alex poured two more shots and handed one to Crissie.

"A toast, to your shit taste in men."

The pair clinked glasses and swallowed the shot. Neither of them even flinched as the strong alcohol traveled through their bodies, a testament to how often they did this.

Crissie was hell-bent on forgetting all about her heartbreak. She had just recovered from the previous one. Since she was finally in a financial position to take Zoe back in, she didn't want to do anything that would jeopardize that. Side by side, she and Alex spent the day serving customers and joking. Crissie looked like her old self again, even if the dark cloud was pushing down harder and harder on her.

—•◦◯◦·◦◯◦•—

A WEEK after she got the money, Crissie had decided to use it since Reece was still ignoring her calls. She'd sent him a text message to thank him, and he replied with only 'my pleasure.'

Crissie couldn't say she was fine without him now because she still looked for him every time a Jeep pulled into the bar parking lot. But she was beginning to deal with it, and that was great. Crissie decided to use the majority of the money on revamping the bar and her house. She wanted it to go to something good and, even if she had to stare at all of the things with the knowledge that he essentially bought it, she was happy to see the bar improve.

Crissie had bought all new bar stools and tables. The place now looked better than it had ever looked, and Crissie loved coming to work. Crissie had also donated all of the old furniture to goodwill. Everything except the chair Reece had sat on when he gave her the preposition to go on the trip.

Although it felt stupidly sentimental about keeping it, she had placed the stool behind the bar. Whenever the bar was quiet, she would sit there and try to forget him. So far, it hasn't worked, and she was just filled with more sadness each time she saw it.

Alex had been a great help when it came to her road to recovery after Reece. Although he realized why she only kept one chair, he didn't say anything about it. He figured that was one part Crissie had to deal with on her own.

Back in New York, things weren't going any better for Reece. However, it made his father very happy to see that he had given up the lifestyle of partying and random women. Reece felt emptier than he had ever before. He was still plagued by thoughts of Crissie. He'd tried to convince himself to call her, but he didn't want to ignite another fire if she had already moved on.

Reece scrolled through his call log. It had been weeks since her last call, one that he declined, yet again. Reece felt lost, and he knew the only way he'd regain his sense of self was by allowing himself the extreme pleasure Crissie brought to his life. Subconsciously he found himself scrolling back to the text she sent almost a month ago.

[07:45] Cristina Fox

'Thank you for the fun and the money. The extra you sent puzzles me, though. I need to know why Reece, please pick up the phone.'

Truth be told, Reece didn't know why he sent her the extra money. He wanted to make her life more comfortable. He wanted her to be happy, and he knew that he could make her happy if he wasn't such a coward. In the weeks since he sent that text, he contemplated sending her more many times. He always stopped himself because he knew she'd never accepted it.

"Just go to her!" James would exclaim every time they talked over the phone or in person. But not even his lifelong friend could get it through his thick skull. "You fly down yet?" Reece ran his hand through his hair, already annoyed by how James decided to answer the phone.

"No, and you know damn well that's not why I'm calling." Reece's tone was short and clipped. His annoyance was easy to hear.

"I don't care why you called. Stop being a pussy and just fly down to Texas already."

Reece ran his hand through his hair again, moments away from hanging up the phone. His conscience haunted him all the time about not going to get Crissie. And now, his best friend had taken up the human embodiment, constantly reminding him of what he was giving up.

"You are supposed to tell me I'm better off without her, not convince me to go, you idiot."

James laughed, "I'm not in denial like you are, Reece. Everyone can see you're miserable without her. Just go and get your woman." Reece resisted the urge to laugh at the irony.

"She's not my woman!" His exclamation came out a lot louder than he had intended. He was trying to get his point across. Still, now everybody outside his office was trying to listen in on the conversation.

"You say that all of the time, but let me ask you this; do you think about her all the time?"

Reece gave a non-committal huff, but James wasn't done yet.

"Do you want her for more than just her body?"

Reece stayed silent on this one.

"lastly, do you see a future with her?"

Reece still didn't respond.

"You don't need to respond or tell me anything. We both know you do, so she's your woman. Just go. You deserve to be happy too."

Reece ignored the idea. "How are the stocks looking?" That was why he had actually called, but it also proved to be an excellent topic changer. Reece and the company had faced one of the absolute worst financial months to date. Even if it was not enough to completely tank the company, they still lost a substantial amount of money.

"Pussy," James announced, "It's stable for now. I'm seeing a lot of people investing back into your company as well as Amazon, so I predict it should pick up within the next couple of weeks. The investments are being made very slowly, so either it is to not draw attention, or it's just small guys trying their luck."

Reece was more than a little relieved. Everything in his life had been an uncontrollable mess. At least if business returned to normal, he would sleep more at night.

"Are you going to fly to Texas now?"

Reece ended the call without a goodbye. He absolutely hated it when James made sense.

CRISSIE WAS worried and close to tears herself as she impatiently waited in the hospital waiting room. Zoe had two teeth that started causing trouble, and her dentist had recommended they be removed. Crissie thought it would be best if it was done under anesthesia, and, thanks to the money she got from Reece, she was able to pay for the procedure.

The irony of the entire situation did not pass her by. Still, she tried her best to keep her mind off everything, especially him, given how much she was stressing about Zoe. A sigh of relief escaped Crissie as the nurses wheeled Zoe out of the theater and into her room. Crissie had to stop herself from running to her daughter, as the doctor came out as well.

The doctor was young, but he was considered one of the best in his field of study. "Ms. Fox, can I speak, or should we wait for her father?"

Crissie almost scoffed out loud. If he was waiting for her father, he'd be waiting forever. "Her father isn't in the picture anymore. How'd the surgery go?"

The young man had a soft smile on his face. "Exceptionally well. We removed three teeth, but as she hasn't gotten her adult teeth yet, it won't impact her forever."

Crissie released another sigh of relief. This was the best news she'd heard in months.

"However," the doctor continued, "Zoe will not be able to eat solid food for a couple of days. You are more than welcome to spoil her with some ice cream and ice pops as it will help with the pain and swelling. Just be careful to not go overboard with sugar. You can also feed her porridge, yogurt, or Jell-O."

Crissie nodded, and once the doctor left, she rushed to her little girl. Crissie sincerely hoped that this would be the last time her daughter saw the inside of a hospital for a long while.

Hours later, Zoe was awake but groggy. Because the minor surgery had been traumatic for the both of them, Crissie decided to host a small party to celebrate the fact that Zoe was so brave after her first dentist appointment and surgery.

The get-together consisted of only Alex, her mom, and a few of Zoe's friends. Crissie had gone all out and made sure to serve snacks that Zoe could enjoy. There were many ice-cream flavors, ice pops, and yogurt snacks, but of course, the main attraction was the ice-cream cake shaped like a giant tooth.

Crissie stood on her porch and watched as Zoe danced and played with her friends, and, despite the smile she had on, Crissie finally felt like she could relax while letting her guard down. As she stood there, her mother watched from the kitchen window, noticing how sadness filled her daughter's eyes.

Her mother wanted so badly to believe that the reason was that Crissie had been worried about Zoe for so long. Still, she knew her daughter had been very different since she returned from her trip with the mystery man.

17

FRIDAY MISHAPS

Crissie woke up the following day feeling a little better than she did the previous night, grateful that nobody saw her little breakdown yesterday. With more pep in her step, Crissie was excited to make breakfast. Today was the first day that Zoe would be waking up in her bedroom for almost a year.

Crissie walked into the kitchen, only to smell somebody already preparing bacon.

"Smells great. Good morning mom."

Her mother stood over the stove, spatula in hand, as she fried up some bacon. She motioned to the chairs by the island counter. "Sit, we need to talk."

Crissie sat by the kitchen island and had flashbacks of her high school days. Her mother would always start reprimands like this. Crissie found herself dreading the talk, even though she was 24 and out of high school.

"Yeah?" her mother looked at her, worried. Her eyes scanning over Crissie like only a mother could.

"What's going on? You've been acting strangely since you got back."

Crissie didn't know what to say. How could she even begin to explain to her mother everything that went down, much less everything about Reece?

"Just tired is all. It's been a stressful time lately."

Crissie hoped her nonchalant attitude would work, but as her mother cocked a brow. She knew it didn't.

"Alexis," her tone was soft and comforting, "I've known you your whole life. I'm going to ask one last time, what is going on?"

A part of Crissie wanted so desperately to lie again, but she knew it was no use. Her mother was bound to find out everything anyway. Like a switch went on, Crissie poured everything out. She told her mother everything from the first time she hooked up with Reece, and she didn't stop until she had said everything that was on her mind.

Crissie surprised herself because, for the first time, she talked about Reece without any tears, and that could only mean that she was slowly beginning to heal.

"Oh my baby," Crissie allowed her mother to hug and comfort her, relishing in the feeling of being in her mother's arms.

Crissie didn't need to hear that everything would be okay. She already knew it. Her mother didn't attempt to make her problems any less. Both women understood that it would happen slowly and that nothing rational would lessen the pain. Crissie had her fair share of heartbreaks, but this one was arguably the worst, purely because she fell in love much faster than she had ever before. Crissie hated herself so much because she didn't tell Reece how she felt when she had the chance, and now it was forever too late.

Everything about her and Reece was passionate and rough, and neither had ever intended for feelings to become involved.

—•⦿⊙·⊙⦿•—

"JUST PLACE IT BACK HERE," Crissie had left shortly after breakfast with her mother and daughter, rushing to the bar just in time for the newest delivery to arrive. Crissie had always dreamt of cooking in the bar and, with the money she got from Reece, she turned that into a reality.

Over the last few weeks, Crissie had bought everything she could ever need to cook and sell food at the bar. That was precisely what she planned on doing as she got ready and unwrapped all of the packaging. Alex was just as excited as she was about the newest adventure they would embark on. So the two of them got lost entirely in getting everything ready and set up.

"So, that goes here, and it clicks in like this. Now turn it on."

The mixer made a whirring sound, and Crissie squealed in delight as she high-fived Alex. "It works-" her sentence was interrupted by a loud knocking on the counter. "We're closed-" Crissie's words got caught in her throat as she laid eyes on the woman holding two large vases.

"Hi, I'm Laura. Alex hired me to spruce the place up with fresh flowers."

Crissie didn't need the introduction. She already knew exactly who the woman was. As the woman reached her left hand out for a handshake, Crissie laid eyes on the beautiful diamond ring on her finger.

"I'm Crissie, excuse me." Crissie didn't shake her hand but instead rushed back into the kitchen. "Florist," she mumbled as Alex stared at her while she ran to the bathroom.

Crissie couldn't think clearly. The only concrete thought that bounced around in her skull was that her ex had already gotten married to this woman. Crissie was suddenly hit by the fact that so much had changed in the year since she and her ex had called it quits. Crissie rushed to the toilet and vomited her entire breakfast out, dry heaving. She knelt, clutching the toilet bowl as her throat and stomach burned.

Crissie didn't quite understand why she vomited, but she felt much better. And after splashing her face with cold water, Crissie had enough strength to go out and face clients again. The day dragged along, and Crissie felt like it would never end. She worked with clients all day, and by the time the after-dinner rush came in, Crissie couldn't stand being behind the bar anymore.

It felt like the walls were closing in on her as she ran to the bathroom, and, in a moment of weakness, she dialed the number that she'd been avoiding for months.

"Please pick up. I need to hear your voice so bad," Crissie pleaded into the phone as the dialing tone rang. But eventually, all she got was his voicemail again.

Crissie slumped against the wall of her stall, sobbing silently so nobody would hear her. It had been almost two months since he sent her the money, and he was still ignoring her. Crissie wanted to move on so bad that she wanted to find somebody who wanted to be with her. But Reece encompassed all of her thoughts and fantasies.

She didn't know how to get over him, and that was the worst part of it all. Because while she sat on the bathroom floor, crying her eyes out, he was probably with somebody new. Crissie hated the thoughts that filled her mind, thoughts of him happy without her, but she knew she'd have to face the truth sooner or later. Reece just didn't feel anywhere near the same about her.

꧁꧂

IT WASN'T long after his conversation with James that he decided to fly back to Texas. In reality, he was kidding himself thinking that he didn't need Crissie. Reece didn't waste any time getting to the private airport and, this time, he had his assistant hire a chauffeur to drive him around.

It wasn't that he didn't want to drive himself around, but Reece knew that he might do something terrible if he had to drive around after a fight with Crissie. He sat on the plane, and he felt jittery and worried for some reason. He didn't know what he would find in Texas. Crissie had been very quiet the last few months, and because of that, Reece was at a loss. He had no clue what was going on in her head and if he was too late.

They landed around dinner time and, although he was a little apprehensive, he directed the town car to the bar. Reece wanted to hop out of the car and run inside when the vehicle stopped, but he knew the thought was crazy even then. So instead, he sat in the back of the car, waiting. Reece wasn't waiting for anything in particular, and his mind was still running crazy.

He'd been sitting in the parking lot for a few minutes when his phone buzzed. He stared at the vibrating phone and the flashing Cristina Fox until it stopped. Reece knew he was a coward, a much bigger coward than anybody knew or that he would ever admit because he was not even 40 feet from the front door of the bar. However, instead, he sat still, waiting for nothing in particular.

Reece sat there for another 15 minutes until he mustered up the willpower to direct the driver back towards his hotel suite. Instead of trying to muster up the courage to go inside and speak to Crissie, he decided to chicken out. He got to his suite, and Reece didn't know what to do with himself. The whole experience taught him one thing; he loved Crissie with all his heart.

Reece didn't know what to do about his realization. It wasn't anything new to him. He'd realized he was in love with her weeks ago before they even left the Olive Canyon Inn. Reece had never experienced feeling this way. All of his life, women chased him. They wanted him more than he wanted them, and now, as he was faced in the opposite scenario, Reece didn't know what to do with himself.

18

PAINT AND DRUNK DECISIONS

Reece sat in his suit and stared at the ceiling. He couldn't believe how easily he had chickened out. Was he terrified to find out she was happy without him, that she only wanted the money and nothing else? He didn't know what to do with himself. It had taken so much to convince him to actually fly back to Texas, but now his fear had him by the throat.

Reece wanted a lot of things, but he denied himself a simple pleasure for the first time in his life. For how long he would be able to keep it up, he didn't know.

On the other side of town, Crissie was getting prepared to implement many changes in her life. The first was painting the color of her house. Crissie stood in the hardware store with Zoe and Alex by her side.

"This one, mommy," Zoe pointed to a bright pink color.

"I love it, but would you rather have your room this color?"

Crissie wanted to make Zoe more comfortable, and if it took painting the house pink, she would gladly do it.

"Hmm," Zoe had her finger on her chin, "yes."

Crissie let out a sigh of relief. "How about this one?" Crissie pointed to a dark grey color.

Both Zoe and Alex nodded, and Alex placed it in the cart along with the bright pink.

Crissie had decided to treat Alex because of the intense labor he was doing for free. She soon started enjoying herself as they laughed and joked. For the first time since he walked back into her life, Crissie wasn't thinking about Reece, and for that, she was thankful. Crissie felt like her old self again. She felt lighter and free. Everything was starting to fall into place. Zoe would be coming home, the bar was doing better than ever, and she was sure she could live and thrive, even with the whole Reece's absence left.

After paying, the trio returned back to her house. Alex and Zoe began painting the front of the house. In contrast, Crissie started to prepare the meat for the barbeque they would have that afternoon. Crissie decided to whip up some frozen margaritas to combat the extreme heat of the afternoon sun. While she set up everything, Zoe started playing music from inside the house and, as they drank, they painted the house.

Crissie watched as Alex and Zoe painted the wall. Zoe created random patterns and giggling as Alex painted over them to create a uniform coat of paint. Crissie loved the view of Zoe playing with a father figure, and, for a brief moment, she was filled with sadness because Zoe would never have that with her biological father. As the sun rose higher, the margaritas flowed, and Crissie was beginning to feel more than a little tipsy. And in her inebriated state, Alex was starting to look more and more attractive. Crissie didn't realize that she only saw Alex in this light as a way to get rid of her feelings for Reece.

The grill hadn't even been lit yet, and the sun was beginning to dip behind the horizon.

"It's sweltering today."

Alex took off his shirt, and Crissie got flustered. Had her best friend always looked this way? Crissie suddenly got a bright idea. As Alex stood with his back to her, she swiped Zoe's paintbrush over his back, leaving a thick grey streak in its wake. Goosebumps erupted over his skin.

"Oh, you're dead."

Crissie giggled like a schoolgirl as Alex came closer.

Crissie began running away as Alex chased her over the lawn. At the moment, the trio was laughing and enjoying everything so much, none of them saw the black town car pulled up in the driveway. A man got out of the car and walked over to where the three of them were laughing. At that moment, Alex grabbed hold of Crissie, and, as she laughed, a flicker of passion danced between them. With both of them leaning forward, they were seconds away from kissing when a throat cleared behind them.

Zoe screamed loudly when she saw the man. Crissie was immediately on guard.

"Reece?" her voice sounded confused as she pulled away from Alex, unwrapping his arms from her waist.

"I should've fucking known," Reece turned and walked back to the car.

"Reece, wait!" Crissie screamed as she ran after him. "Please let me explain. It's not what you think."

Crissie was stone-cold sober now as she placed herself between him and the car. She needed him to understand that he didn't see what he thinks he saw.

Reece was having none of it as he walked past her and got in the car. Crissie was crying hysterically as she pleaded with him, "please, Reece, nothing happened, I promise you." She pounded on the window until he rolled it down. "Reece, please, what you saw was nothing."

Reece ran a hand through his hair, "nothing? Nothing! you fucked me when you were in a relationship."

"I'm not. Reece, please, let's talk about this."

Crissie wasn't calming down, and Reece wasn't about to back down either.

"How fucking could you lie like this? Was the money all you saw?"

Crissie hiccupped as she cried, "no, I only saw you. I wanted to spend time with you."

She wanted to scream out how much she loved him, how much she felt for him, but she knew he wouldn't care or believe her.

"I'm so sure about that. You look very heartbroken about not seeing me for months."

Crissie cried even harder, "I was, I still am. Reece, I tried to call you so many times-" she was about to explain her feelings when he cut her off.

"You have a fucking kid, or did you just happen to forget all about it while you were sucking my dick?" Reece was furious. He couldn't believe what he had walked into.

"I wanted to tell you about Zoe. Trust me, I did, but I never expected to catch feelings for you."

Reece laughed ironically, "does your fucking husband know you have so-called feelings for me? Or is this just another way to get money out of me?" Reece motioned to Alex as he walked towards the car, a crying Zoe in tow.

"Reece, please, it's- ... this isn't what you think. Just let me explain."

Reece looked her square in the eyes. "You've done quite enough already." Reece turned towards Alex, "Enjoy her, fuck knows how many other men will while you're married to her." Reece spoke to the driver for a moment, "stay the fuck away from me."

With that, he pulled out of the driveway, "Reece, I love you!"

Crissie screamed it at the top of her lungs as the car sped down the street. She prayed that he heard her. She prayed that he'd turn around and come back so she could explain everything, so she could make everything right again. Crissie stood in the middle of the street, sobbing and crying as she felt her knees buckle beneath her. But before she could hit the ground, Alex picked her up.

Alex pulled her close to his chest, and she started hitting him with her fists.

"This is all your fault. How could you try to kiss me? I am so stupid, and now I've lost him forever."

Crissie was crying and slurring as Alex dragged her and Zoe back into the house. Crissie was still spewing profanities at him as he led her towards the couch.

Zoe watched her mother screaming and crying with tears in her eyes, "Mommy?"

The moment Crissie heard the soft words, she stopped screaming and motioned for the girl to come closer.

"It's okay, my love. I'm sorry I scared you." Crissie was still crying as she held the girl, both of them now sobbing.

"Come, Zoe. Let's go to grandma's house. Mommy needs a little time to sleep." Alex whispered to the girl as her mother let her go.

Crissie watched them drive away, her heart shattering into a million tiny pieces. She'd managed to lose the man she loves and scare her daughter all in one day. Crissie walked upstairs and locked herself in her bedroom, effectively putting herself back at square one.

19

REGRET AT ITS FINEST

C rissie hadn't left her bedroom since everything went down yesterday. She didn't want to eat or drink. She didn't want to do much of anything, really. Crissie was furious with herself for not confessing her feelings earlier. She was furious with Alex for trying to kiss her, but most of all, she was furious that Reece hadn't given her time to explain herself. Crissie knew that it was all a massive misunderstanding. She couldn't blame Reece for what he saw, but she could blame him for not wanting to listen to her.

Crissie had tried calling him. She left hundreds of missed calls and voicemails during the night, and when she even tried to message him, he'd blocked her number. Crissie felt even worse than she did when her ex broke off the engagement, and she could freely admit that she was more in love with Reece than she had been with any man before him. Crissie wanted to scream at how happiness had eluded her once more, but instead, she stoically stared at the ceiling. Every inch of her being wished this was all one bad nightmare, which she'd wake up any second in Reece's arms.

Crissie didn't know what came next. She didn't even know how to process everything that went down, and, in a moment of absolute regret, she tried calling him again. "You've reached the voicemail of Reece Hunter…"

Crissie hung up the phone, unable to control the pained sobs that escaped her chest. She knew she had to find a way to explain things to him, but she was at a loss about how to do it.

Reece sat in his suite in pretty much the same condition. He didn't know what to do. His worst fears had been exceeded. Nothing inside of him wanted to believe that Crissie was the type of person he had just experienced, but he knew it was time to move on. He felt puzzled about what he saw. How could he be stupid enough to fall into her trap? Reece watched as she called again, which marked 30 calls since he left the previous night.

On the one hand, he wished she would just stop. On the other, he wanted to hear her out. He wanted so desperately to believe that she was telling the truth, that what he saw wasn't the true reflection of what was actually going on. But he had seen enough to know that wasn't the case. He saw how they acted around each other, and he would've seen them kiss had he not interrupted. He felt stupid and used, and that brought even more questions to the table.

Did her husband know what she was doing behind his back? Reece was sure he must've. It was most probably his idea too. Using his wife to get their mortgage paid off. Was there even a mortgage to begin with? Or was this just a scam they ran on wealthy businessmen? Alex had known he had money. After all, he had seen the black card when he signed him up for the classes. Reece was getting more furious as time went on. How didn't he see the signs?

Then she had a child as well. How could she raise a daughter if she couldn't even keep her hands to herself? He couldn't believe just how much he had missed. Reece was hell-bent on erasing every part of her from his mind. He'd spent weeks dreaming about her while she was happily playing house with her husband and daughter. It was infuriating, to say the least. For the first time in his life, he actually dreamt of being with a woman for reasons other than the physical.

"Ms. Dixon, I need you to adjust my schedule." He didn't care about the time in New York. He just needed to make sure he wasn't around this part of town ever again. "Push meetings back and arrange for all foreign travel to be completed within the next few months. I will be back in time for our trip to Dubai, schedule each and every other trip to follow immediately after."

After conferring with his assistant, he was certain that he would be busy for the following year. That he would never have to come back to this part of Texas ever again. Reece was satisfied with his decision, and he tried his absolute best to sleep well that night. Still, every dream was plagued by pictures of Crissie and her happy family.

CRISSIE FOUND herself sitting behind the bar. The business was slow, and it did nothing to help keep her mind from Reece and everything she lost. She didn't even want to be here, but Alex had begged and pleaded that she stand in for him while he went on a date. Despite the hand that Alex played in her losing Reece, she had forgiven him. After all, he promised it was just the alcohol that caused him to act like that.

Crissie believed him. After all, it was a lot easier than admitting she actually wanted to kiss her best friend. Ally played with a shot glass as she tried thinking about anything that would make her happy but, even then, Reece was at the forefront of her mind.

"A round of cocktails, please, beautiful lady."

Crissie came face to face with her mother and aunt Layla, a group of their friends accompanying them.

Crissie put a smile on her face. "What's your poisons tonight, ladies?"

Each of the women gave an idea, but Aunt Layla put a stop to it all. "We'll start with *Sex on the Beach*. Lord knows none of us to get it anymore."

The ladies all chuckled at the joke. Most of them started finding seats, leaving only Aunt Layla and her mother at the bar.

Crissie tried to make the drinks, but as she started, her breath got caught in her throat. Crissie suddenly felt overwhelmed with memories of the day she had met Reece for the first time after their one-night stand. Crissie tried her best to keep her composure as she half-heartedly listened to her mother and Aunt Layla's conversation.

Every now and then, she would laugh along at a joke or make a comment when they asked for her input.

"There you go, six *Sex on the Beach* cocktails. That will be 24 dollars."

Aunt Layla took the money out of her wallet but stopped before handing it over. "You forgot the cherries. That's the best part."

Crissie tried to laugh it off as the memories shattered her heart even more.

"Are you okay?" Aunt Layla asked as Crissie put the cherries in each of the glasses.

"I am just tired." Crissie could see that her half-assed excuse didn't fly, but her mother kept quiet.

"In that case, come shopping with us tomorrow?"

Crissie wanted nothing more than to decline the offer. She had major plans with her bed, wine, and some ice cream, but one warning glance from her mother was enough to make her utter the words, "I'd absolutely love to. Pick me up at nine?"

Both of the ladies walked away. Her aunt was quite happy that she convinced Crissie to have a girls' day with them. Crissie absolutely hated that she had agreed, knowing full well that it would just cause everything to be worse.

20

SWEET REVELATIONS

C rissie had known regret, she'd spent enough time dwelling in it over the last year, but there were very few things she regretted as much as going on this shopping trip. The women had spent hours browsing through stores, and none of them had purchased a single item.

"We're just walking through, and then we'll go back and buy the items we like. This way, we're surely getting the best prices."

Crissie had heard this response about ten times already, and she was seriously debating buying the items for them just so they could go home already.

Crissie dragged her feet as she walked behind them, feeling like she was back in high school and that her mother had forced her to come along. Crissie longed to have Zoe with her, but the little girl was at daycare, and Crissie was promptly refused when she requested to bring her on the shopping trip. Crissie had a pretty good idea why. She really hoped that the women would not corner her for an interrogation about what happened with Reece.

Her mother noticed how Crissie was acting. How she was walking without her usual pep, and she longed to have her daughter back, the daughter she had before all of the heartbreak. Her mother had seen firsthand how strong Crissie could be. She went through childbirth and single motherhood on her own before all of the heartbreak. In her mind, she knew something terrible must've happened between her and Reece. Crissie hadn't even known him half as long as she did her ex, and yet, this time, Crissie was in a lot more pain.

Her mother knew Crissie would fight when they asked her about the whole ordeal, and that is precisely why she had crafted such a genius plan. In reality, the entire shopping trip was a ruse, and it had just been to get Crissie out of the house and out into a place where she could speak calmly about what was going on.

"How about lunch?" Aunt Layla had announced.

The idea made everybody grateful, but not anywhere as much as it made Crissie happy.

The women sat around a table, but the conversations were strained and forced. In reality, it was a miracle that Crissie had not caught on to what was happening.

"How are you, Crissie?"

The entire table went silent, impatiently waiting for her answer.

"Good, I've been very busy at the bar," her tone was short and clipped. Her attention focused on anything but her mother or the situation at hand.

"How about your personal life?"

Crissie immediately realized where things were headed, but she decided to play dumb. "There's nothing to tell."

Nobody looked convinced at her answer.

"Are you sure, sweetie?" Crissie knew Aunt Layla was

just trying to be nice. They wanted to help her, but there was nothing anyone could do.

Crissie stayed silent, just nodding her head once, her attention still focused on the menu as she flipped through.

"Don't be disrespectful, Crissie," her mother reprimanded.

Crissie snapped as her mother made a tsk sound.

"What do you want me to say, mom?" her voice was raised and her eyes wide. "Want me to say that it hurts to breathe? That I see him every time I close my eyes? That my entire being hurts because I love him more than I've ever loved any man? Because I do and because of one fucking mistake, he doesn't want anything to do with me."

Crissie lowered her voice as the first tear slid down her cheek. "I hate talking about how I fucked everything up once again. How happiness escaped me and left me back at square one. I am a crying emotional mess, and because of that, I can't look after my daughter. So like I said, I'm okay." Crissie slapped the menu closed, her tears now flowing freely over her face.

The women around the table stared at each other in disbelief. Crissie had spilled the beans much quicker than they anticipated she would.

"What happened, my dear?"

Her mother's voice was soothing, and it only made Crissie cry harder. Through her tears, Crissie spilled all of the beans, from start to finish. The women all stared at each other. Nobody could believe what Crissie had just told them.

"Go and find him! Make him understand what he saw."

Crissie wanted to. She wanted to do it so bad that every fiber of her being screamed for it. But she had no idea where he was or if he'd even flown back to New York yet.

Aunt Layla dialed a number and spoke on the phone for a minute. "He's still here. The plane has not departed."

Crissie remained in her seat, flipping through the menu again. Even if she was to go, what would she say? Where would she even find him?

"Would you just go already?" Aunt Layla tried to convince her, "it's clear you love him, now go and tell him exactly that!"

Crissie remained seated until both her mother and the rest of the table collectively yelled, "GO!"

Crissie speed-walked to her car. She really hoped he was still at the hotel. If he wasn't, she had no idea where she would go looking for him. As she pulled up to the hotel, she could see his town car and chauffeur still parked in front of the building, and a little bit of hope bloomed in her chest.

Crissie rushed into the building just as Reece exited the elevator, his bags in tow.

"Please let me explain," she begged as she stood in front of him, her breath ragged from the jogging.

Reece wanted to refuse, but still, he led her away from the lobby and into a business lounge off to the side.

"My flight leaves in an hour. You have 15 minutes."

Reece was short and disrespectful, but Crissie didn't care. She was just happy to get the opportunity to explain to him what was going on.

"Thank you." Crissie took a second to compose herself as Reece stared impatiently at his wristwatch.

"14 minutes," he announced.

Crissie took a deep breath. "I was engaged a year ago to a cop in town. He was great to me initially, but as time progressed, he got more and more distant. People told him all sorts of things, that I was a whore and that I'd been cheating on him during our relationship. He began to hate

Zoe because she wasn't his daughter. He then cheated on me and left me, with lots of bills to pay and one hell of a broken heart." Crissie stopped to take another breath.

"That explains almost nothing, 11 minutes."

Reece kept his eye on his watch. He knew if he stared at Crissie for too long, he'd forget all about what she did. He needed to hear the truth. He needed the closure, even if he knew he'd be leaving without her and that this would be their last time together.

"I understand, and I'm getting there. I spent eight months getting over him. At that time, Zoe lived with my mother. When I met you, I was desperate for money. It was only my second week out in society after everything went down. That's why I was giving the lessons."

Reece looked at her for a moment. She was battling to keep the tears at bay, but he refrained from trying to comfort her.

"Alex is a good friend of mine. We've never dated or been together, and Zoe is not his daughter. I am not married to him, and the only person I had any feelings for during our trip was you."

Reece searched her eyes for any sign that she was deceiving him, but the only thing he found was raw honesty.

"I never meant to hurt you. I fell in love with you on that trip, and I was so heartbroken when you disappeared that I turned to Alex for comfort. What you saw was only one drunken mistake. I didn't plan on it, and neither did Alex. I don't love him. I only love you."

Crissie hoped that she was making sense, and she prayed he understood what she was trying to convey. Crissie was crying now, her tears running over her cheeks as she begged him with her eyes.

Reece believed everything she said, and he wanted nothing more than for her to be telling the truth.

"I will be the first to admit that I originally said yes because of the money, but that wasn't the only reason. You looked so familiar to me when you stepped foot in the bar, but I couldn't place you in my memories. But when you started telling me about our hookup, it became clear who you were. Five years ago, you were the only one-night stand I'd ever had. I had just gotten out of a relationship, and I wanted to let loose, so I never asked for your name or number. Three weeks later, I began to feel sick, and at first, I thought it was the flu, but I found out I was pregnant with Zoe. I wanted to find you, to tell you so bad, but I didn't even know where to begin looking for you. You were just some guy from New York." Crissie took another deep breath.

"I didn't tell you about Zoe because, at first, I wasn't sure how you'd react, and I'd been raising her fine on my own. But as I got to know you, I realized that you'd be a great dad, and then I found out about how much money you had. I didn't want you to think I was lying because I wanted your money."

Reece felt one stray tear run down his cheek.

"I ... I have a daughter?"

Crissie nodded, looking down at the floor.

"I wanted to tell you, and I am so sorry..."

Reece stopped her mid-sentence. He decided to stop being a coward. He could tell she was telling the truth even if he had no guarantee. He wanted her, and he wasn't going to let her go ever again.

"I should've listened. I was so afraid of loving you that I ran. I ran until I had nowhere else to go. When I saw you with Alex, I felt relieved through the sadness because if you were married or in a relationship. I didn't have to face my feelings for you. I love you, Cristina Fox."

Crissie stepped into his embrace, and he kissed her tenderly. All of their frustration, anger, and pain vanished, leaving only love behind. Reece pulled away lightly and whispered in her ear, "Want to go for a ride?"

EPILOGUE

Crissie stood on the balcony of her New York home with a cup of coffee. Her eyes focused on the two kids playing with Alex in the pool. Crissie wasn't entirely sure what they were playing, but her kids laughed loudly, and their happiness was all that mattered to her.

She'd only woken up a few minutes ago, alone in her bed, but, by now, she was used to Reece going to the office in the early hours of the day. It always bothered her when she woke up alone, but with Reece, everything was different. She was different. Crissie felt grateful that Alex came to visit because he kept the kids occupied. She could sleep in. As she lifted her cup, she caught sight of the diamond ring on her finger, and she was hit by how surreal it felt. It felt like yesterday she and Reece had screamed at each other in front of her house back in Texas.

Crissie couldn't believe how far they'd come in the five years since that went down.

"Mommy," Noah yelled loudly as he spotted her. He waved from the pool.

Crissie waved back as she walked back into the house.

She laughed softly to herself. Reece had tried everything in his power to have Noah's first word be 'dad,' but it was to no avail. The little boy had proudly exclaimed, 'mommy.' Reece wanted to be unhappy about it. Still, he couldn't bring himself to once he saw the absolute joy it caused within Crissie.

Crissie was happy, for the first time in her life. She was totally and irrevocably happy with how her life had turned out. Crissie started packing bags for the kids, herself, and Reece. When they got engaged, Reece had promised to work remotely for two weeks every second month. Those two weeks were then spent in Texas, in their house while she worked at her bar. Reece knew it would take a lot out of Crissie to say goodbye to everything she knew, and therefore he compromised. As they say, a happy wife enables a happy life.

In the past five years, Alex and Reece have also become good friends, especially after Alex got in a committed relationship and eventually got married. Crissie knew her relationship was secure, and there was no room for doubts and distrust, which was why she believed they worked so well. Crissie looked at her watch when she finished packing and realized it would only be a few more minutes until everyone would get together at their house before they all flew down to Texas.

Crissie had a big surprise planned. Initially, they would all just spend a few nights in Texas to celebrate her 30th birthday. Still, there had been some other developments over a few weeks.

Crissie placed a hand on her growing stomach. She hoped that Reece would be surprised when he found out, but she also knew he'd been suspecting she was pregnant since she had her first bout of morning sickness. Crissie got changed into comfortable clothes, much to her father-in-law's dismay. He'd always hoped Reece would marry a woman that always looked like she had just stepped off a runway.

Despite Crissie not being exactly what everybody imagined, they all adored her. Crissie was perfectly imperfect, with her wild hair and yoga pants to her house that was only mostly sparkling clean. She was happy, and so was Reece, and to their families and friends, that was the only thing that counted.

Crissie walked downstairs just in time to catch James and his girlfriend as they came in through the front door. They didn't knock on the door, and Crissie loved that their house was a place people felt comfortable in.

"Hi," Crissie hugged both James and his girlfriend Drew.

"Has he noticed yet?"

Crissie shook her head, "he has a little idea, though."

They all shared a laugh at Reece's expense.

James and Alex loaded all of their bags in the car while Crissie got Noah's car seat ready with the help of Alex's wife, Bethany. The six of them had spent a lot of time together. They had all become quite close over the years. Crissie rechecked the time. Reece was 15 minutes late, like always. Because everyone was ready to go, she was just about to call when he sped into the driveway on his vintage Harley Davidson Dyna.

"I'm here!"

Reece greeted James and Drew before walking over to the kids. He kissed both of their cheeks and slyly handed them candy.

"What do we do?"

Both kids looked back at their mother briefly, "don't tell

mommy." Zoe exclaimed loudly, her eyes going wide as she realized her mother heard her.

She motioned to her mother to keep quiet, and Crissie couldn't help but laugh. The kids took it so seriously, and Reece loved how they felt they had a secret with just him.

Reece ruffled their hair as he went up and kissed his wife. "Hello, my beautiful wife."

Crissie wrapped her arms around his neck as Alex, James, and the kids made disgusted noises. They all got in their cars and drove off towards the private airport.

CRISSIE WAS tired after the flight. Her body ached as jet lag hit her hard. It was weird to her because she usually had no issues with jetlag. As soon as they reached her home, everybody set out into their usual bedrooms. And not even an hour later, Crissie's mom stopped at the house to see her grandchildren. Crissie had kept quiet about her newest pregnancy. She wanted to tell her mother in person before she told Reece. She didn't want anybody to know before Reece and her mother. Still, Alex had seen her throw up, and he realized it immediately. James and Drew had realized it when she refused a glass of wine at dinner.

It amazed her how Reece still hadn't realized yet, or maybe he did. He just wanted her to tell him herself, but either way, she was grateful that she would get the opportunity to tell him this time around. When she got pregnant with Noah, Reece had realized before she did, and she completely missed out on the chance to make a big deal out of it.

Crissie stood in the kitchen and baked. She missed baking in her kitchen a lot, and nobody thought it was suspicious that she insisted on baking her own birthday cake. Her mother sat at the kitchen island with a cocktail, watching Crissie as she colored the batter to her birthday cake.

"You're pregnant?" Her mother whispered the question loudly.

Crissie nodded with a smile on her face. "I'm going to tell Reece later today."

Her mother wrapped her arms around her, unable to contain her joy. "That's so great, Crissie."

The two women sat and talked for a while as the cakes baked in the oven. Reece would periodically come into the house to make sure his wife was alright. Crissie could tell he knew, but she was going to surprise him regardless.

$$\text{---}\bullet\mathcal{C}\mathcal{O}\cdot\mathcal{O}\mathcal{O}\bullet\text{---}$$

LATER THAT NIGHT, as they all sat around the barbeque, Crissie brought out the cake and set it down in front of Reece.

"I propose a toast and, as the birthday girl, you all have to allow me." Crissie started, "I want to toast the best husband and father to his amazing four kids..."

Reece looked confused. "Four?" he cut her off mid-sentence.

Crissie nodded with a bright smile.

"Yes, we're expecting twins. I'm almost 17 weeks along."

Reece had known she was pregnant, but he kept quiet because he knew how much she wanted to surprise him.

"I know that you had a feeling about it, but I wanted to surprise all of you. The cake is colored on the inside. It correlates to the genders of the babies. Red for girls and green for boys."

Reece couldn't help the smile on his face as he cut into the cake. Swirls of red and green stood out.

"We're having another boy and another girl."

Reece almost tackled Crissie to the ground when she said it. He was completely overjoyed. Crissie had filled all of the parts of his life that he didn't even know were missing. Reece stood with his arms around Crissie, staring into her eyes as all of their friends and family clapped and cheered.

Zoe and Noah cheered as their Nana explained that they would be getting another brother and sister. Everything was great, and for once, there was no bad turn ahead, no other metaphorical shoe that had to drop. No, they had been through enough together, and now, they could enjoy the fruits of their love.

As they kissed under the fading sun, they both realized that life couldn't get any better.

ABOUT THE AUTHOR

Rose M. Cooper read her first novel when she was eight years old. Since then, she has read tens of novels and twice as many short stories. She, however, did not discover her special knack for writing romance fiction until a decade later.

Now a full-time author with a specialty in contemporary romance, Cooper writes sensual yet relatable love stories designed to hook her readers at first glance. She views writing as another outlet to creativity, and thus has no intentions of setting down her pen just yet. There are many intriguing love stories to be told, and Cooper is set to tell them all.

She hails from New York and currently makes her home in Copiague, New York with her husband, her black cat and her Maine Coon cat. When she is not writing, you will most certainly find her around computers or getting her nose stuck in a book.

facebook.com/RoseMaeCooper

twitter.com/rosemaecooper

instagram.com/rosemaecooper

Sign Up For My Newsletter To Receive New Release Updates & Specials!

rosemaecooper.com/newsletter

THANKS FOR READING THIS BOOK. PLEASE CONSIDER LEAVING A REVIEW WITH YOUR RETAILER!

Made in the USA
Columbia, SC
30 September 2021